MY HE
IS OPENING

Evelyn Conlon

Attic Press, Dublin.

Contents

DEDICATION
To my mother and father.

My Head is Opening

Louise was married and she had had several children spaced over eighteen years. She didn't have energy or desire to socialize, any more. Her husband did though. But she didn't mind too much, now. If he was away, he was away. It didn't matter whether he was out working or out socializing. She had become accustomed to being on her own. The slight madness that hits new mothers who want and want and who remember themselves as they were before, had left her a long time ago. She had become so that the craving obsessive need for adult company, symptomatic of her early marriage, was only a memory — a bad memory. She had learned, by eliminating certain responses, that the needs which advertised sanity among adults could be diagnosed as unhealthy, if mothers had them. Prisoners — she thought. But prisoners kept a little dignity. They were never asked to love their gaolers. They were never expected nor believed to like solitary.

Eventually Louise got tablets. Small white round

ones with a line down the middle — the kind used by the medical goverment as tension management agents for people like Louise. Women who couldn't or wouldn't say 'I like it. This is what I expected, even what I have always wanted. I hope nothing ever changes.' She hadn't wanted the tablets at first, but after some years of trying to beat defeat she regularly welcomed some dulling of the thought process. Thinking had got her nowhere. Better finish it, kill it.

Louise started going to bed at ten o'clock at night to help things slip by a little quicker. She didn't want all life to slip by. Just the part that had to be got through until things got better. One day she would savour time again — she was nearly sure of that. Louise was bright. Often she would lie in bed, denied the drift that comes before the turn over into dark lands. On nights like those she welcomed the sound of Daft Dan as he invaded the avenue with his maniacal laughter. The straight damp avenue whose houses showed neither joy nor crisis. Ever. Dan walked the avenue every night, issuing forth a wild throaty laugh as he strode down the concrete strip. Each laugh sounded as if it was the last. Its echo remained for some minutes, hitting off the shiny windows and becoming faint as a baby's laugh in the next room. Then silence. The righteous shuddered in their sitting rooms to think of what might be in the unknown. Louise always waited without breathing, hoping for another sound. Then if it came — sometimes a long hollow sound aimed at the sky — she exhaled with it. The time always came when his voice was too far down the avenue for her to hear. Then she would relax and would thank him for something — she wasn't sure what, courage perhaps — and sometimes a few measly inadequate tears would come.

One night Dan's laugh was particularly crystal. The wind carried it clearly when he could only have been as far as the avenue traffic lights. That would mean a long communication tonight. As he neared Louise's house the sound melted, as she always pictured, and subsided down his throat. For her, it was a burn, a hiss, a comfort. Nature was working, somehow, in strange places. Louise reached to him in the dark as she always did and this time their spirits touched somewhere in the silence above the black avenue. Dan turned to her window. Now it was clear where the answering call always came from. Never before could he pinpoint the house because his echo had not hit her window directly. He felt the warmth. Some presence. Some soul, whispering 'It's all right. I understand too. Be free. Be here.' He stopped. What was this care that came from that house? Who was it who understood? He turned to the room across the street as if to salute the presence behind the window. His head threw itself back, the stars flashed for him, and he let his laugh out free. A long clear note, a plea, a teardrop. Again the unkempt sound came — this time a victory call. Louise moved to her window. She had never seen Daft Dan before. She was curious. She pulled back the curtains and preened her eyes. There he was. A tall man, aged maybe sixty. He had a handlebar moustache. She had expected that. She supposed his eyes were green, and poignant no doubt. She stood transfixed as he puzzled over the clarity that had come to him momentarily. He opened his lips and pleaded. Louise watched his laugh forming. She stared. She heard a car. She saw Dan fall, before she saw the car or heard the shock of metal on his flesh. A low whimper moved from his lips. Louise moved herself from the window and ran down the stairs out the door across the street. Her pink cotton nightdress with the red flowers, billowing around her, lent a certain homeliness to the bloody scene. She bent over Dan, but she knew he was dead. She touched a red gash, reverently. She looked at his face. It was healthy. She had expected that too. He wore a dark blue paisley scarf. His moustache lay over his mouth adding an elegance to a sharp broad face. She sat on her feet, watching him, refusing to believe that he wouldn't laugh again.

It was a close night and muffled sounds were added as people came from their houses. Some gathered in small groups near their gates, whispering; others strode confidently towards what they perceived as the centre of action; as the ignorant will, but then turned quickly when they saw the face of Dan. All eyes were turned from Louise and Dan. The people fussed over the driver of the car because he wasn't dead and he was young. He asked for a drink and someone ran to get it for him. Ran. Ran for the hero — Louise mused bitterly. Her eyes pierced through him. An ineffectual looking boy who was probably showing off. He was the centre of attention as he explained to all what had happened. Louise would not strain her ears to listen. She didn't believe him and she didn't want to hear excuses. The crowd interjected repeatedly to ask if he was sure that he was all right. He was. He was. A bit shook, but all right, thank you. He did not ask about Dan and the crowd were careful to shield him from the view but they needn't have, because he never once turned in the direction of the corpse. One woman came to Louise with a blanket. She handed it over and said in a low voice, 'You will know what to do. I am sorry. Did you know him well?' Louise folded the blanket neatly and laid it over Dan. No one turned to see that the dead body was now a dark blanket. Louise turned for comfort, when the task was done, but the woman was gone.

The biggest circle of people parted as someone of importance arrived. It was a man in a brown suit. His yellow shirt had a narrow faint brown stripe and his brown tie was matched with a subtle yellow fleck. The crowd knew importance when they saw him. He strode to the driver, patted him on the back and in a loud confidential voice, assured him 'I saw the whole thing. How ghastly for you. I believe that the man who stepped out in front of you was quite mad. Everyone here knows that.' They all nodded. 'You should sit down in one of these open houses while you are waiting' 'Yes, yes,' they chorused. 'Of course. We were just going to say . . .' The driver and the brown suit moved towards an open door followed by the other shifting bodies. Louise stood up carefully. The crowd didn't notice her move. She walked across the path that they were making to the door and planted herself in front of them. She drew her breath. They watched her. She spat once, then twice, at their feet. They halted sharply, eyed the woman in the long nightie, and cleared their throats. Brown suit put his arm protectively on the driver's arm, like a clamp, and ushered him quickly past Louise, furtively through the door, in case there might be trouble. Anyone who had seen the spitting hurriedly followed the driver and brown suit, to offer further support and to ally themselves with the healthy. Three or four people stayed, their eyes slanted elsewhere, not seeing Louise or Dan. They muttered to themselves. Louise resumed her position beside Dan. An ambulance arrived. Efficient men jumped out, strapped Dan to a stretcher, handed the blanket to Louise and drove off without a word.

Louise stumbled through her door and made herself tea. She told her husband, when he came home: 'You know the man who laughs all the time. You know him. You must know him.'

'Can't say I do. I've an early start tomorrow.'

She secretly attended the funeral of John Francis O'Driscoll. He hadn't been called Dan after all. There were six people there. The mourners did not know each other. The priest didn't single anyone out for the particular handshake. Nobody cried and nobody went for a drink to drown any sorrows.

Some weeks later Louise slumped. She didn't want to believe that her only soulmate had been an anonymous man who walked down the street bellowing laughter at everyone. A mad man. But he was't a mad anonymous man. He was Dan. She couldn't tell anyone how she missed him. She lay in bed earlier even than before and longed for sleep so that the hand-grip of the brown suit and driver would stop menacing her. She stopped getting up from bed. She láy for weeks, sunk in some well, not trying to get up or out. From there they sent her to therapy, after her husband noticed that she didn't even answer him any more. The therapist did his best with the little perverted knowledge that he had. He asked her if her mother had been cruel to her. She looked at him and thought — poor child, is that all he knows. He asked her if she had loved all her children equally. She narrowed her eyes and stared past the impudent pup. He asked her if everything was all right in her marriage. 'What?' she shrilled at him. He waited. Now he'd get to the bottom of the problem. He tapped his pen, pleased with himself, but nothing more came. Just the one 'What?' He sighed. He stammered through the other rituals but could get nowhere. This patient was a complete blank and he felt that she wanted to stay that way. He gave her more, stronger tablets. Something would work, he'd make sure. He hated failure. Sometimes her husband collected her from the therapy sessions. That was nice because it meant that she saw someone during the day. He was a good husband, Louise thought, if she thought about it at all. He would collect her. He would drive her home. They would come in through that strange door that must be hers, into what must be her kitchen. She would make him tea. It was her kitchen. She knew where everything was. He would drink his tea and then go back to work. She felt privileged while he was there, at lunch-time. But then she was alone again. Better really. She didn't have to talk and she could have a little sleep. Just a short sleep. Once or twice she woke up laughing — short laughs, that never really got far enough down her belly to be any relief.

It was a morning in June. Louise remembered it well. Everyone was gone for a long day. Longer than normal, but she could never remember why exactly. She dragged herself from her bed when the door had closed for the last time, and opened the cabinet for her tablets. She moved the other medicines aside carefully but her bottle wasn't there. She had left them downstairs. She went downstairs. But her tablets weren't downstairs. They must be behind the other medicines upstairs. She went upstairs but they weren't there. They had to be downstairs. She went downstairs and looked in all the possible places. Maybe they were in her bedroom. But she never left them in her bedroom. She moved from upstairs to downstairs and up again and down again. She removed everything from every drawer and every cupboard, carefully at first but then more roughly as she became agitated. She began to shake. Her head began to pound — pound in her ears — the chairs and windows moved away from her. She held onto the kitchen rail and hissed at herself 'Damn you. You fool. Where did you leave the bloody tablets? Think. Think. Think, you fool. What are you going to do if you can't find them? Think.' But she couldn't think. 'Where does that leave you?' she sneered at herself. She started with the last step that she could remember and tried to move back over the night but couldn't think beyond her usual routine. And she had obviously not kept to her usual routine, or she would know where her tablets were. Muzzled. Her brain was muzzled. Finished. She started again but three hours later she had still not found her tablets. She wilted down on the top step, her shoulders fallen, and stared at the back of the outside door. There was a coloured glass panel and a clock which gave notice each day of the number of milks required. She looked at it and looked again and stared but saw nothing that could give her comfort, reason or sense. She would move to another place in the house. Perhaps that would help. The bedroom. She hauled her body up, holding on to the bannisters, and stumbled to the bedroom. She staggered by the mirror. It showed a shaking figure with a grey face that passed without looking at itself, as it stumbled on and on and on. A decision. Should she get into bed with her clothes on? Should she put on her nightdress? The cotton nightdress with the red flowers. A decision. Yes. She would take off her clothes and yes she would wear her nightdress. Her legs supported her by digging firmly into the iron of the bed-edge as she hauled her clothes off. The rest of her body leaned towards the bed, impatient now with human habits. At last she was there. Her shoulders collapsed from rigidity and her head sank through the pillow on to the floor, through to the ground outside. She lay there. She had no tablets. She would have to think. A small tear came to her right eye and moved down her face into her ear. She turned on her side and the tears got spilled by the movement. Silent drops. Louise rarely cried. She lay there half-surprised by these tears. Welcome little jewels that softened her head and spread her creaking headache into a duller, more manageable pain. Slowly she started to sob. Real sobs. Sighs. She began to see a little. She cried then — really cried — for herself. For her lost self. Her spent, wasted self. Her lonely self. People died never knowing loneliness like hers. She cried and cried and began to know that she never wanted to stop. She had so much to weep for. She rested for periods during which people passed through her head — anonymous people — who had stared at her in public places over the last decade, thinking to themselves, 'She is killing herself and she doesn't know — poor thing.' Of course she knew it. She sneered. Who were these people? Self-important people who thought that because they knew how to live and look, they also knew how to be. 'What was I thinking???' She cried some more. The people didn't stay long enough for her to put a finger on solid knowledge or to get an answer to them. Her head was muzzled. She was outside. Perhaps she was the answer herself. Two things were certain. Dan was dead and she couldn't find her tablets. Louise wept some more.

Later in that long day people came home to Louise's house and watched her. They peered at the sogging heaving mass and wondered. She still cried and they wondered about her, then wondered what to do about her. Her husband Tim came home. He got the doctor and got tablets. But Louise screamed 'No, no, no — I do not want a tablet. I will not. I find some ease coming. Give me a while.' Her husband looked at her — saturated eyes — and shrugged his shoulders. 'We will see.' She cried her vicious tears for two days and two nights, gulping for air, as mounds of disappointment and bitterness eased through her eyes. And all the time there was someone downstairs to bring her tea.

After that they took her to another therapist. She didn't talk to him at all. It wasn't that she wouldn't, it was just that she was thinking about something else.

The night when her storm had begun to quieten, a picture came before her. It was of herself and one of her children. Her first daughter. The daughter was ten. She wanted to remember what was before. But there was nothing before then. Now today sitting here in this office the fuzz was clearing. Louise heard none of the therapist's questions. She was answering her own. Her husband collected her. He pressed her — 'What did he ask you?' Louise looked at him sadly. She knew that she would disappoint, as she had often done, when she was a child. 'I can't remember.'

'What do you mean you can't remember. You've only just come out of there.' He was agitated and raised his voice. 'I hope he can do something for you. He costs enough. Did he give you better tablets?'

'Yes.' Her husband was afraid to ask if she would take them. She didn't care, one way or the other. She was tired caring. Something was happening to her. Her head was remoulding itself, inside. She was seeing people.

Her daughters and her sons trooped on. People she'd never really got to know. They were babies. She fed them, was good to them, controlled them, loved them and then they grew up. Grown people now. She should feel guilt about them. She felt nothing. But before them there was only her and her husband. And her husband. Who was he? He was twenty-two years old then. He was Tim Sorohan. Timothy Sorohan. A gorgeous-looking man. Imagine she had thought him a man at twenty-two. But then she was twenty. She thought he had dreams, real dreams — not the run of the mill stuff — but she couldn't remember now what they were. They had married. Louise had hated her wedding day even more than she expected. She never went to weddings now. She was excused, but for many years she hadn't been. Every wedding was worse than the last. At first she didn't enjoy them because she was always sitting beside a stranger. As she got older she resented being expected to consider these celebrations as enjoyable outings. She didn't know why she felt this way. Timothy settled quickly. He got a promotion as a wedding present. He talked a lot about children — too much, the young Louise thought. She was hoping for some time. Time for what? New brides were meant to become new mothers. Why wait? Louise, why wait? So she went the way. The first child was the hardest. The others were graded comparable degrees of hardship, pain, fright or hope. It was hard for her to remember ordinary days of those baby years, because she was afraid. Afraid of what to do with those memories. Remember the day a passer-by spoke to the baby in the pram. Who was it that was in the pram? Anyway the baby, whichever of them it was, was delighted. But the passer-by rushed on. Louise was left with the disappointed screams of a baby — as well. Why couldn't that passer-by come back and finish what was started? How dare these people smile and walk on! What was she to do with that memory? Remember seeing married women speeding past in the backs of cars, holding babies, looking vaguely out passenger windows. Louise had looked vaguely back at them, uneasy at possible comparisons. But no. She was different. After all she had known other dreams. She had tried fiercely to hold onto them for later. Those women didn't look as if they ever had dreams. There was the very bus stop where she had sworn that nothing was going to change, when she was eight months with her first. And Timothy had promised. At that time she still read. But more babies came and her husband started talking to the shadow beside her. She read less. Books dissatisfied her and left her yearning. There were no books for this side of things. Another baby. Her skin was getting older. Dull backache, all the time. One tooth was bad. Ordinary, ordinary days, punctuated by a funeral, a relative home from America, Christmas. On these occasions she perked a bit because people really looked. They asked sincerely 'How are you getting on?' They didn't wait for an answer but judged instead by how she looked. Another baby. One time her mother and her aunts took all the children. Tim and herself went away for a weekend. They said almost nothing. He drank a lot.

They never did it again. That sort of thing only led to trouble. Louise now knew the meaning of certain emphases — 'What would *we* be going away for?' She stopped reading. Todays had to be endured. Tomorrows might be different. But they never were. Springs, autumns went past. She hated autumn most. It goaded her in subtle ways about the darkness ahead. Winter at least had no cover-ups for its death rattles. In winter, she woke in three stages. Some part of her body rubbed another part — What have I touched? Am I real? Does it have to happen? Then to a higher consciousness out of the dreams, where she recognised herself and what had happened. Then she woke. Always woke. Once she got to the second stage she always woke. Some people were glad, each morning.

Timothy and Louise reached the house. She had not spoken once on the journey home. He reckoned that she was worse. He said so, in a harsh voice, and then softened to 'We'll see.'

Louise wasn't worse. She was thinking. Weeks later she was still thinking. Autumn wasn't so bad. Before eight children there was Timothy and Louise. Before Timothy and Louise there was Louise. She remembered now. The more she thought the more she remembered. Pictures of herself reading a book. Another picture, reading another book. Why had she stopped reading? Why had Tim not done something for her? Why? He could have. He had peace and time to think. Why hadn't he? She hated him. No, hold on. She couldn't start saying things like that. She calmed. It didn't matter. But it did. Who was Louise? She was a daughter. She was twelve. She wrote in her essay — 'When I Grow Up' — 'I'm not sure what I will do but I do know that I won't do certain things, like getting married and/or having children.'

'And/or,' they laughed. They tut-tutted for a while.

Her mother said to callers 'Did you hear what Louise wrote in her essay?' Always with a nervous admiration in her voice. Louise grew in fits and starts, reading books to suit her moods — romantic, sharp, doomed, hopeful. Books where people chose, prison books, busy books, quiet books. Stories where no one chose, where everything happened in deluges from the sky and everyone was forced to go on, regardless. At twenty, she thought she was grown. She had a boyfriend. She was getting a library job, at last. In the new library. But the job fell through. Such a simple thing really. She read the books where no one chooses and felt so bad she went to romances. Her boyfriend began to appear in a different light — celestial. He took on new qualities hitherto never possessed by twenty-two-year-old men, and certainly not by Timothy. Louise thought, 'I can live on my own. I can choose. I do not need to get married. I have lots in my life — books and other things . . .' And then she thought, 'I don't have to prove it. I don't have to be different simply because I could be. Why should I? Who would believe me anyway?' So they got married. Timothy had asked several times and was relieved that he wasn't going to have to pester her. Anyway she was going to have time. Time before having children and she would look for another job in a library. But Timothy settled quickly.

Louise, meet Louise.

She heard voices from lost women relatives and from books where people choose.

Louise started with a disused book. Months later the childhood where she was allowed — no, expected — to learn, was less far away. She walked down Florence streets for a morning stroll before packing her bags to go to Venice. She dropped into Paris on the way back to see how the politics were in that city. She moved to poetry on contemplative days. When she shopped in the supermarket she didn't see the crowds of children, didn't hear the voices of too many people — no, she moved in the pleasant parts of imagination as she put her ailed body and mind back on the earth of the thinking living. Louise would have liked to tell Tim but each effort to do so ended in grunts and silence. All he knew was that she was not taking tablets any more and seemed to be all right at the moment, but of course you could never tell with that sort of thing. She did talk a lot about books, but books were books after all. She also talked about herself much more than before, but Timothy Sorohan, as he was now, was not one for either of these topics.

'I would love to go to Italy.'

'Italy, are you off your head?' Timothy nearly sneered. 'You always wanted too much. Others were content. Others were content.'

'But I did what was expected of me.'

'Yeah,' he said grudgingly, 'but you always expected more. Too much ...'

Louise stretched, and said softly 'No harm in expecting.' Timothy sullenly asked what had been wrong, really wrong, with her life.

'I wasn't impressed with it,' she nearly giggled. As good an answer as any.

'Impressed?' he bellowed. 'Who ever is?' He looked at Louise and thought, she is, yes she is worse than before.

When summer came Louise went to Lourdes. It was easier for Tim that way. Next year she could go to Italy. For sure, this time.

I Deserve a Brandy and Port

I've wanted to do this for a long time. Start drinking on my own on a Saturday afternoon and keep drinking until closing time, if necessary and if I'm fit. Closing time — the hour when drinkers are thrown out into the dark, some to be happy, some to sink down into overwhelming, grating despair, battering all around them in their slump. I've always believed that one Saturday like this would find me a new world that I know is out there somewhere. Or else it would make me happier with my own. I want to see what happens. I'm not looking for a man or anything like that. That's the whole point of this. I may look as if I am. What woman would do a pub crawl on her own all day on a Saturday unless she was looking for something? But I'm not. They'll just have to believe me and I know that it's not going to be easy for them. But I'm not looking for a man. I just want to be a free woman around town for a day. And I can't be free if I have someone else with me.

Not really free. Other people always affect the way you answer questions or ask your own. So I'm alone. Drinking the piece out. Moving from one pub to another. I have to move because of the hassle. That's only fair. I have the rent money in my pocket and that would be enough to keep me drinking for a week. It's a dicey business, but now that I've started — it's 5.30 — I can't go home. If I went home now I'd fall asleep, waken up at midnight with nowhere to go and I'd get depressed. So it would be better to persist. Persist regardless. But I've had some weird conversations already. What will it be like by 11.30? But this is life, isn't it? This means something. The first drink was strange. I actually thought — no, I can't do this. I cannot brazenly go up and order a drink all the while looking nonchalantly around for an empty seat, pretending that I am looking for my friend who is obviously late. Who do I think I am? But I did it.

'One pint of Harp please.'

'Yes love.'

Handed over my money, got my change, put it in my pocket and sat down. Just as if I was waiting for someone. It didn't take a fidge out of me. I was so obvious though, now that I think about it. Nervously sitting with my pint among the men and their pints and the couples, of course. There are couples everywhere I go. They're even there in my dreams. Bloody couples. Kissing, fighting, or disintegrating with boredom, not a word between them to say. That's when I began to feel good, when I thought about that. Here's me. I'm not part of any boring old couple. I can sit here and drink all day if I like. No one to tell me what to do or to force me, just by their presence, to consider what it is they might like to do. The pint was funny, though, because I tasted all of it. It wasn't as if I was talking to someone and the pint was being drunk without me noticing because of the chat. No. I was tasting every mouthful. I began to feel really good the more I looked at the men with their pints and the couples. There was one couple in the corner. Heterosexual couple. He had a broken right arm so she was cutting his sandwiches into little manageable pieces. She occasionally held his pint to his lips, presumably when his left arm got tired. It's true. I saw it. The strangest thing about this public unveiling of their normality was that neither of them seemed at all embarrassed. Ordering the second drink was easy. I had a few moments of doubt before I did it. Perhaps I should go to another pub? Wasn't I pushing it a bit? There was a slimy creep in a suit eyeing me. Fuck him. I went up to the bar brazen as hell.

'Another pint please.'

'Yes love.'

Love, my arse.

I sat down. Then it happened. A man out of nowhere plonked himself down beside me. Well, it's a public house so there's not much I can do about that. I haven't rented the place for a private party, so I'll have to put up with him. I tried to ignore. Don't even think the word 'him'. I looked out the window with a distant look — one, I fancied, that poets maybe or recently deserted wives might have. Narrow pupils widening slightly at the wonder or horror of some new thought. That's a daunting look. No one would interrupt that. But I couldn't keep it up. It's very hard on your eyes because you can't blink too much or you lose the effect. Then I tried other looks, but I was fighting a losing battle and I knew it. So did he. And he knew that I knew. I had a half pint left. I thought to myself — Not yet. I just couldn't take an argument yet. It's not fair. I can be very silly at times. I imagine that there is such a thing as human fairness. I sometimes forget that I am a woman. Silly of me really. So I stood up and finished the drink in two, three gulps. It nearly sent my head flying but I got myself collected and left the bar without even glancing at my table-mate. I thought to myself — Lady you're a genius. I made for the next pub. I bought a paper along the way. This place is grand. Two or three people that I vaguely know came up to me but only stayed a minute or two because I had the paper to protect me. I glanced at it every now and again. People usually take the hint. I drank two pints of water, as well, in that pub because I was worried about getting drunk. People might think that I was mad. I was again joined by a single item of manhood. This one was more straightforward than the last one.

'Would you like to share your depression with me?'

He was obviously dead trendy. A depressed trendy. Nothing worse.

'I beg your pardon,' I said as if I'd spoken that way all my life.

What I meant was — There's more than one way of trying to get inside a woman's knickers and I know what you're up to, depressed or not. Baby. By the end of my drink this man was really bothering me. He told me that he knew that I had a right to drink on my own. If I really wanted to. No one knew better than himself. I ignored him. No one knew better than himself. Wasn't he a feminist.

'No such thing as a boy feminist,' I muttered, even though I was ignoring him.

Weren't all his sisters feminists? They became feminists after he brought home all those books. It was the best thing that ever happened this country. That whole movement was great — you know.

I was so rude to him, you'd think he would have learned, but no. I rustled my paper, I read, I glowered, I didn't speak, I read again. Reminds me of something else but I can't put my finger on it? But he kept on. By this stage I couldn't concentrate. I glared again.

'My mother as well. My mother was also a feminist.'

That nearly got me interested.

'Of course you see, my father was . . .'

I didn't hear because of my next glare. He kept it up — a continuous audible stream of words. Then he started complaining about his wife. Fuck this for a lark. I left. Next pub.

I decided that I wasn't going to move again come hell or high water. Deep down I knew that these elements were the least of my worries. I settled myself in a comfortable corner re-enforced now with two magazines. (There comes a time when all reading material looks like the prop of a lonely person — nothing else — when it's produced in a pub particularly, but I couldn't very well afford to think about that.) I made it clear to all patrons that I was on my own and was here for the duration of the night, or as much of it as I could stand. The new confidence had come with the drink. The place was getting busy. People meeting people. All talking to each other. Human nature as it is I suddenly longed for conversation. Just a little conversation. I've only myself to blame. I'm the one who thought it would be a good idea. Right, I'll start a conversation. I'll talk but I'll be careful. The problem is — the other problem is — to tell you the truth I'm getting a bit drunk. Say if I start a conversation with someone really nice, can I trust myself? Will I be able to control myself? Will I be able to get through it without making a pass at him. You know what men are like about women making passes at them. I won't worry. By the looks of things someone really nice is elsewhere tonight. So I started talking to this man. I kind of like him. It's now 9.30 and I've had plenty of pints. I'm beginning to get very clear in my head. I can see why women are bitter or something like that. I'm thinking how clear-headed I am. Drink does that you know. You can spend hours marvelling how clear-headed you are. Mornings you usually forget. Anyway I'm talking to this man. I think I like him but I'm not absolutely sure. At least he's letting me talk. Unusual. We're talking about marriage now. I hadn't meant to talk about those matters. When I'm drunk I prefer to talk about politics or something like that because it's safe. No one gets randy talking about politics. Next thing I know I hear him saying, 'I haven't got along with my wife for two years.'

I can't bloody believe it.

And I was just beginning to know that I liked him. Does he think that I started drinking yesterday or that I was born with an inbuilt sympathy detector for men or whatever other cliché a man like him would know? 'You must be trying to chat me up. Men always say that when they're trying to chat a woman up. Married men that is.'

He was flabbergasted at my cheek.

'What fascinates me,' I continue, 'is that they always say two years, never one, never three. I wonder why that is. Do you have any ideas?'

He winced.

'I feel sorry for you,' he said in a low menacing voice and then, warming to his own menacing, 'You are so bitter and unreasonable. You must have had some terrible experiences in your life.'

He says that he feels sorry for me. Hah! I give my short sarcastic laugh, the one that worries even me. It makes me feel sometimes that I'm getting too cynical. He's talking again in response to my laugh.

'I feel sorry for you. I feel sorrier for the men that have to meet you. I feel even sorrier again for the young men coming in ten or twenty years time if the girls are going to get even worse with all this lib stuff. And they are going to get worse. Mark my words. Unless there's a stop put to it.'

What with the drink, I was beginning to feel sorry myself for the young boys coming up, but it was for a different reason. I couldn't figure out whether I should walk away from him, which is what I felt might be the wisest thing to do — get up and slide away when he was mid-sentence, him being so het up he wouldn't notice — or whether I should bombard him about his wife, who was no doubt answering the hundredth nightly request for a drink of water from his offspring at this very moment. Give it to him right between the ears. I often do the wrong thing when I have drink taken. I think that I've got my images perfect so I blabber my mouth off. Then when I see the astounded murderous looks I stammer 'No, no. Cancel that. What I meant was . . .' But there are some spoken words you cannot cancel.

'Sorry love, what did you say,' he asked me.

'Nothing,' I said.

'Well I can't see why a man can't discuss his home situation without being accused of . . .'

I began: 'I knew a woman once, a fine woman, who shadowed her husband all their years together. A strong shadow, so strong that few people noticed how she depended on the sun for her very person. A shadow nevertheless. Sooner or later shadows go completely. Too much rain, too little sun and they disappear. Often very suddenly and unexpectedly ... More shadows come back when the sun comes out again and few people notice that these are not the original . . .'

I glanced at him. He was pale. He had the same look as a fellow that I asked one night how did he know that he was the father of the children that he was bragging about. That night, as soon as I had said my piece, I knew that I had landed the poor woman at home in serious trouble. Tonight I couldn't figure this fellow's reaction. Had I jolted him into thinking that the woman at home might leave him — a thought that he had never ever known before — or was that thunder I saw on his face, because he couldn't understand what I was talking about and thought that I had changed the subject deliberately. This is getting dangerous. I wish we were talking about politics. Thank God for politics. I looked away at the far corner of the room, waiting, thinking to myself — You bloody fool. Eejit. Now smart alec. Get yourself out of that one. I didn't know if I was thinking about him or me. I wondered what they'd do in the pub now if I had a heart attack. What do they do with customers who have heart attacks during drinking hours? Do they get mad with them for putting others off their drink? I wouldn't go into a pub for some time if someone had a heart attack beside me. At least not that particular pub. I think very fast when I have a few drinks on me and when I've just put my foot in it. I turned my eyes down to the floor shuffling all the time, still waiting for his prissy reply or else for more tears. I looked up and Jesus Christ who did I see coming in the door but 'Would you like to share your depression' himself. I jumped up and ran towards him. His face lit up when he saw me coming. I grabbed him, pointed to my seat and roared at him: 'Listen there's a man over there who needs you badly.'

He took me seriously and while the two of them were eyeing each other with rampant suspicion (men are not terribly fond of each other) I ran out of the conversation and the pub.

I thought to myself — Lady, you deserve a brandy and port after that. Pints are only for people who don't have the rent in their pockets. Not that I had all the rent left in my pocket at this stage. I strolled into the last pub fifteen minutes before closing time. I'm taking them by storm now. I had two B & P's. No one bothered me. I got high again on silence. I left before the barmen started screaming like ignorant gulpins, and made my way home by unsteady foot.

I've turned the key. To tell you the truth once again I'm ossified now. But I've got home haven't I? Safe and sound as a bell. Do get into the bed. The sofa might look all right now, but you'll waken up in a single knot with a pain everywhere. Here I am now. In the bed. My bed is a lovely bed. It's big — so I can stretch both my arms and legs in splits dance fashion. Didn't I do well to get here. I had a great day. I think. Perhaps I meant it to be different. What am I forgetting? I am forgetting something. What am I thinking about? It was lousy. But I sort of enjoyed it. I must do that again some other Saturday because I know that there's something out there that I'm missing.

As Good a Reason As Any

I had you because of your father. It was because of where I came from. He took me (not just me, me and your sister and your two brothers) in after the divorce. It's not often you'll get a man like that. That was three years after the divorce. I had given the children one total year each of my life as well as the rest of it. I was ready for comfort. I had come from my grandmother whom I had seen crying only once when I handed her my child, her first great-grandchild. She said it wasn't fair. Once, someone coming on holidays asked her if she had a car so they could get a lift around. She wrote back no, but she had a washing machine. Once she went to her daughter's house where there was a dishwasher. She said, we do them in the new sink at home. I didn't want to betray dignity like that but there I was, divorced. My aunts and uncles had gone to Mr and Mrs competitions and laughed coyly when asked which room the wife took off her nylons in and how the husband cut his toenails, as if they were modern visionaries. Things had disimproved over the generations.

Your father wanted a child of his own. After the divorce I'd been sitting one day with my brother outside the hotel waiting for our grandfather. He'd said, there's a wedding. I could see that. He wanted me to look and approve. He left the car to get the paper or so he said but my self, that was vicious by now with goading, knew that he was going to look to see who was getting married. Your father was a relief after all that.

When I was first married they used to ask me how I was doing, then they changed it to how are you both. If I had the questionable advantages of marriage they weren't going to let me away with thinking that I was still me. Then they'd try to make me work up some sympathy for the next-door neighbours who were still single, just to test. All I could feel was envy. Your father said, when I met him three years after the divorce, that I'd taken the woman out of women with my cynicism. I was flattered because he knew something of me, even if he'd got it all wrong, and I smiled and fell for him.

We lived happily for some time, he bumbling around an area that he hadn't ordinanced. He had been written into the script late. I would meet my next-door neighbour, who was happy that year as well, in the morning or the evening, and we would greet each other with large smirks as if we were hiding some secret from the rest of the street. Lovely day, isn't it. Beautiful. Big smile. Awful day. An evening for the fire. Grin. Then your father began to look wistfully at your sister and two brothers, ah but they're not mine. I'd feel for him the same as I used to feel for my unmarried neighbours, but he was convinced. His seed or nothing. I thought about pregnancy. I knew he didn't. Because he had no children of his own. Then I remembered that my husband hadn't thought about it either even after the experience of the first, because he didn't have to have them. I got into a state then because I'd always wanted to believe that some part of my husband could be locked away like Oliver Plunkett's head, kept free of my disappointment. I could fill up my despair hole with another child, surely. Trouble with mothers is that they fall for everyone — all their children that is, even the ones they haven't got. Yet. It's always yet when they get to that stage. Being was all that my other children wanted from me, doing didn't come high on their list. Motherhood was threatening again.

I remembered being sick. Worse still I remembered being tired. Not a whiff of energy left as the new generation collected all the goodies that it could from me, so that it would have an easy growth in the water I too provided. But being sick makes you appreciate little things — health, bedroom slippers, spouses, lovers — things like that. You forget that you wouldn't need bedroom slippers all day if you weren't sick. I felt guilt about your poor father who hadn't a child of his own, even though some days I knew that I was really a pedestrian-crossing, skipped and trampled on heartlessly by offspring as they moved to something else. Mothers are like that. Guilty, I mean. I remembered one day that I'd looked out the window, for fifteen minutes, and when I had landed back among my care, zoomed in like superwoman, they had surrounded me with toy soldiers, all of them pointing their guns at me. I was hurt.

I thought again about pregnancy — the effect it would have on my body structure, you know the muscles inside and out, the womb, the stance, the bladder (I was crossing my legs daintily already when I coughed or laughed too much, what would another one do?) but most of all my back. My poor poor back. But I had been excused from the gym class of the world by this time. I belonged to no team and your father had been good to me.

I dreamed a lot about women. They were whispering me on. They'd all had their babies. Some of them had been thrown out of their homes for it. Some of them had murdered their babies and themselves. Some of them had given the babies away but they were all still egging me on. Next morning they would fade into one woman, perhaps a stranger I'd seen on the bus one day, who had too many children and was expecting again. She lived in a new country where people now smiled encouragingly at their two children and asked them did they have a nice day at school and taught them to be positive about themselves before the money would run out. I had sniffed, disgusted at her. Get out of the hole. The war is over. But in all honesty, she couldn't.

I myself had been in parks with children, not talking to others with children. Creating allies might cause a war. But I had to leave myself with some beliefs. I even knew that I shouldn't trust men who were out all day, but I did.

My second son was going to dancing in the New Contemporary School that used to be my friend's kitchen before she got divorced and moved to a smaller house because of the poverty. I could have done with a bit less starvation and a holiday, but time was moving on. I swore that if I had a child, this time I would tell it the truth of where I was reared. In the end it was easy enough and what wasn't easy about it you don't need to know yet. You don't mind me telling you this . . .

In Reply to Florence

Mona was sorry that she was on crutches but she tried not to think about it because she would not be in Italy again for some time, if ever. She had broken her leg one week before the holiday started but wisely they had not cancelled. The pain was bearable for someone who was as used to pain as she was after several miscarriages, one pouting serious child, a varicose veins operation and a collapsed uterus. Her uterus had collapsed from too much dilation.

But these were distant worries. She and Des had just booked into a cheap clean hotel near the Piazza del Duomo. Florence at last. Rome had been interesting, but they had wasted it on the ferocious rows of a middle-aged couple flung together for three days when they were now used only to compartmentalised time sharing. Rows about money, about how to get places, about souvenir shops. She didn't want to spend time in souvenir shops, he did. Map reading. She didn't believe in maps or map reading, he did. In Rome she had seen a young man and woman kissing. They were brazenly feeling each other's nipples. She was revolted but also seized by a shock wave of envy. She had hurried Des past them for fear he would notice. The next day, after sex but before compatibility, they passed two jaded tourists kissing with their tongues. Des teased her 'What are they doing.' She was aggrieved and disdainful of his childish familiarity with her. But those three days were over. Now that they were used to each other again, all would be well. It must be, it must be. Because it was not often they could have a holiday. Des's family was looking after the child, now fifteen years old. Mona was an only child, her parents were dead, she had no cousins or aunts. She dressed in grey-green colours, flat shoes, confined tailored skirts and hygienic white underwear. She had never been contaminated by knowledge of or sympathy for unmarried mothers, lesbians or the world.

Their window opened onto a scene of pigeons, Italians on motorbikes, tourists and other wooden shutters. Sunshine poured down on the picture. Mona was happy. Des was pleased. He was always pleased when everything was running smoothly. Even minor emotional disturbances put him out of gear. They went for an evening walk, past the Piazza del Duomo. They looked up at Giotto's bell tower and Mona made a note to climb it tomorrow. She would like to see Florence from the sky. More so than Rome. The people were walking slower here, the young peacocks in the Piazza della Republica were more ostentatious, yet they shrugged easier that all was not fair in love.

Compatibility was settling on Mona and Des. The quiet acceptance that they could not have what they wanted, in life, in love. That happiness was a myth, that love was a transient trick. Mona fingered her wedding ring. Buying it was supposed to mean something. It had cost a lot. She was on her own among strangers. Her

husband was with her but she didn't know him very well.
Even yet. They had a meal in the Casa di Dante and went
back to bed early. Tomorrow was to be a full day. Mona
had read the guide-books. She wanted to see everything.
Des would follow her because he knew that she was the
expert here. He didn't realise that he knew this. Perhaps a
more relaxed form of holiday might have helped them
better to know themselves at fifty, but that would have
pre-supposed plenty of time and youth and also that they
wanted to know each other better. They both slept well.

Tomorrow that was now today led them through
gallery after gallery. They took the tours by the book,
stopping sometimes for short drinks or ice-cream. They
sneered inwardly at Americans, two of whom, at this
minute, were having a loud conversation about a statue.

'But what does it mean?'

'It must mean something.'

They surely could not have come so far to find even
one statue that had no meaning. So they tried . . .

'I know. That looks like John the Baptist — that's one
of the angels playing the harp . . .'

'That's not a harp!'

'No, and that's not an angel, it's some saint.'

'What are they *doing*?'

The statue lounged in contempt. They walked on.
Another American stopped her.

'Excuse me.'

'Yes?' said Mona, flustered.

'You're American. Thank God.'

'No, actually, I'm not.'

'Well you know what I mean.'

A map was unrolled hastily.

'Can you tell me how to get to . . .?'

Mona decided that she wouldn't even try.

'Try the taxi rank.'

'But when we say we're American they shrug their

shoulders.'

'I wonder why,' Mona thought.

She linked her arm into Des's — the cold clinging of strangers in a foreign country — and hurried away. They walked into the Uffizi gallery to feast. Mona needed art. She needed it to fill her. Seeing made her other senses work. She could feel then. She could believe that she was more than a space in a cavity. Des appreciated art, he didn't need it. They thought that they understood each other. They had a sparse meal for supper. Mona did not want wine because it would lift her spirits to another area that had nothing to do with what they had seen today. She wanted to stay with portraits of other people. In her real life she was surrounded by chilly cliché-diseased people who, like herself, had to notch up importances for themselves. But she could never collect everyday experiences or acquaintances in order to make her less afraid of death. In the suburb where she lived at home people climbed ladders in little steps, the right covering on the couch, lamps on low tables with glass tops, chance meetings with powerful people. The women in the suburb were just peasants, dragged from their fields into this cold trick. What had run through their mothers for blood had not left them yet, but they hadn't got this far up the ladder to grumble about necessities that were missing. It would be years before one of their daughters would look back. There were no old women walking up and down the road talking to themselves. They were safely away somewhere else. These new suburbs wouldn't tarnish their image. Thinking daily about these things predisposed Mona to liking Florence. She sighed after supper. The galleries had been wonderful. The sculpture. The churches. The pink hue around the Piazza del Duomo. She went to bed ticking the day off in her diary with as much delight as if she still had to live it. She was partly embarrassed by the pleasure of such a day.

'We don't make love very often, Mona.'

She was shocked. What was he talking about. Oh yes. She shook herself. She owed him a response.

'I wonder why? I suppose it is because . . .'

She looked at Des. I've had your child, she thought. I could still have another of your children. What more do you want of me, just now when I'm in Florence.

'I wonder are other people like this?'

Mona didn't know.

'What should we do about . . . eh not . . . making love often enough?' she asked, forcing herself to mind.

'Just do it.'

'But that surely is not the answer. Why do we not want to love each other more?'

Des shrugged. He tried not to talk personally any more. They made love, he with the impatience of the sort of man he had grown to be, she with seething resentment. He slept. She moved back to the galleries with an ease that she had learned from other women. Minor satisfactions interrupted her daydreaming, the fact that he knew as little Italian as she, his frustration at not being able to order, to command with his usual ease. She knew better how to get on without language because she was used to long-distance signals that were often disrupted or lost, because even her own tongue did not speak for her. She thought of Shelley — did his first wife commit suicide or was she thinking of the wrong man? Why didn't she know? She moved uneasily in the bed. It didn't matter that she didn't know — he was a great poet. She fell asleep. And dreamt.

Paintings walked into her vision. The Old Man. He was sympathetic. He had wondered and thought. He had learned. He was understood. Beside him was a coy lazy woman or at least those were her defences because she was stripped and had become nothing but her breasts. There were more like her, they had become nipples or thighs. The Sabine women were destroyed. They were raped again and again, every time a tourist ogled behind the sympathy. The men had books, the women had plumes. Men with granite bodies moved around her dream flipping aside fading pale women whom they didn't even see. Mona was sinking. This wasn't her world. She ran around frantically looking at the tapestries to see if a woman had done even one of them. Surely the tapestries. But men stood at the top of each of them calling to her, 'Come see my work, come to real places.' She fled from the tapestry room but was confronted by a tour guide from Fiesole. He was hushing a group of tourists into a sitting position. They stared at him and did as they were told. Mona stood rigid. He looked at her but decided to ignore her. She watched as he spread his arms over a forum that had risen behind and underneath him. His arms flailed wider getting longer all the time as he gathered together thoughts of immensity from the past. He embraced all of the single days and single chores of every man that had helped build this forum. For a moment his arms slunk dejected right to his sides when he talked about the slaves who carried the stones, who broke the stones, who died underneath the stones. Then he lifted them again solemnly to lay the poor slaves to rest with dignity. Mona had thought for one moment that he was going to mention a woman. She would have liked that. Perhaps he had thought about it because his eyes flickered to her but she shyly dropped hers because it was too brazen of her to expect. She walked away disappointed, looking back at the forum, at the stage, suspiciously, as if she had just caught her mother out in a lie. She started to cry. The David loomed before her and sneered. She dried her eyes, swallowing hard, ashamed in front of this marble marvel. She apologized. He shrugged and walked into a room where a huge feast was laid on a table. All the men were there — Michelangelo, with his arm proudly around David, Rembrandt, The Old Man, Leonardo da Vinci, five of the Medicis, thousands and hundreds of them. She had never seen so many men before. All of them were congratulating each other. She walked away like a child. Someone patted her on the head. She heard a loud laugh. It was the David. He was clinking his glass with her husband Des. She shook herself — was her world really only a figment of her imagination? Perhaps she was not real at all. She heard a voice, 'How large is the universe? Are the known measurements reliable?' She half woke. She wanted something better than being. What was better than being? Wake up, she urged herself, this is just a waking feeling. Busy yourself. The edges of the dream fell away, the outer rim of the Colosseum, the gaping height of Giotto's tower. She was more than a body performing daily tasks, eating, sleeping. She grew pansies with faces as elusive as Leda in Leda and the Swan. She grew sunflowers. The chance to put away her dream receded. She was asleep again. It was Christmas morning. She was sitting on the bed wakening her child with presents. Her mother sat beside her watching, bewildered at Mona as a mother. She had forgotten that Mona had a child. 'Wake up. Look what Santy brought you.' The child sat bolt upright, waking too fast. His eyes lit up, then red anger and tears. 'I don't want stupid toys.' She remembered. She had meant to tell him the truth — 'Mammy, is there such a thing as Santy?' he bawled. Mona frantically whispered to her own mother. Do I tell him now? Is he old enough? Her mother asked what age he was. Mona said nine. When was he nine? September. 'I'd say it would be all right.' If only she'd told him yesterday. It seemed so odd to declare yourself a liar so soon after lying. The dream collapsed. She woke fully, thinking vaguely about lies and half truths, about religion, about art, about men. She dressed quickly, dreading that she would waken Des. She left a note and went to an early café where she ate a seasoned omelette. Sixty Americans getting ready for the day, eight inches apart, flocking around, pressing into tour guides, were out already. She didn't know what was wrong with her. It must be the dream. She would go for a walk. That would help her. She looked at the guidebook to Florentine *man and his* Art. Stop being so silly, she told herself. She walked down a narrow street wishing that she had no pain in her leg and that she could forget her dream. Everywhere she turned there was a penis. Door posts, umbrellas, whole houses. She blinked hard. There was still a man standing in every inch staring at her. She was crying. She must have a temperature. Please, please, she whimpered. Please. She staggered into the Gallery of the Academy and Tribune of David. Perhaps it would be cooler in there.

When they arrested her she laughed at them. They screamed at her in Italian the whole way to the police station. She smiled. Art. I was doing performance art. They threw her in a cell staring at her, shouting at her. One of them lifted her crutch to hit her, another stopped him. When her husband arrived he was wearing his suit and tie. As soon as the *carabinieri* saw him they got a translator. The inspector and he shook hands, sympathy being the password. They told Des of how she had been hitting David with her crutch when they apprehended her. She had hit him first all over. Then she had poked at his genital areas, but her most vicious attack was for his head and mouth. Luckily she had not the strength to do any damage. Why did Mona do it? 'No why,' she chanted like a child. 'Because,' she brazened like an adolescent. The adult finally said 'I must have cracked up.' That satisfied the police.

Because of Des they escorted them both to the train station not the airport. They trusted him to get her away by train. He informed her coldly that he presumed she would allow him to see Venice as it was on their original itinerary. 'Yes, of course,' she answered quietly, like an over-reprimanded child. She hated every cubic inch of it, every dollop of coloured glass, every accusing shop window. Slowly they boarded the train home. Venice ran into Milan. Large previously precious names were worth only momentary glances. Milan ran into Vergiate, a small village where a woman waited on her bicycle at the level crossing, visibly peeved, because the train was delaying her on her journey to the shop. Vergiate was now a named place for Mona, who had her nose pressed against the window. A young man was arrested in Lausanne at 12.40 am. Des ordered Mona not to look out the window 'Or would you like to draw more trouble on us?' Hours later she ventured apologetically, 'You won't tell anyone, will you?' He looked at her with disgust. 'As if I would.'

Transition

Maisie Ryan was carefree, twenty-two, and not very sensible. Why should she be? Time enough for that later. She lived in a rented suitable house in a quiet, wide Dublin street. Suitable that is for her parents, Mr and Mrs Ryan. (She barely noticed the house in her quick visits there, between social outings and work.) Mr and Mrs Ryan could call on their daughter any time they were up in Dublin and were always assured of a welcome. The other three people who shared the house were indeed much more sensible and suitable than their own daughter, as far as Mr and Mrs Ryan could ascertain, but no matter, she was young yet and had a few more years to play with.

Meanwhile, as the various mild worries of parents about children floated around the universe, Maisie was getting ready for a party. She was going with — not *with* for Christ's sake, along with — Adrian Pollack. He had the in to this arty oldish party. At least he said that it would be arty. She chose the clothes to wear confidently, flicking through the trousers and the odd dress. Off-pink linen jeans with two narrow tabs catching the leg material at her ankles. Pale canvas top matched with brooch. A scarf thrown around her neck, taken off and thrown around her neck again in a more casual manner. She was the perfect balance between the dressed and the natural. She approved of the vision that flashed back at her from the mirror. She could imagine herself naked.

The party was passable. Maisie had enough to drink. She wasn't falling around the floor nor singing nor crying — just enough. She had a warm sexy feeling. It was growing all over her body. It was in her ears by now. She danced. She had a private stretch and grin as she moved herself into the rhythm of the dance. She went to the powder room — hah — ran her two hands down her body and went back to the dance floor. Then she saw him and got warmer. Funny how she always saw someone eminently fanciable when she was feeling like this. Could it be that her own feeling made him fanciable? Never. That was too cynical for Maisie's quarter-grown world. She was standing beside him, in a matter of minutes, having worked herself through a routine of minor movements. She didn't believe in waiting. His name was Manus. He worked as a vague something or other with IC, a computer firm, he travelled a lot and was hard to contact. That would mean that he would do the ringing. Well Maisie was willing. He was laughing as much as she now. They played expertly together. This was magic. It was obvious that both had the same intentions, so they could dally a little. No need to rush themselves on each other. Better to savour the slow-glowing delights of easy success, without making the success seem cheap or unsophisticated. They moved from giddy to casual teasing, from familiarity to brief shyness. Around three o'clock their passion could hold itself in check no longer. Light touches, any movement — none were free now. There was a painful straining of their bodies that they could not control, even if they wanted to. People magneted together. So they went to Maisie's suitable house, to her suitable bed and spent the night on that other level where bodies dig, hold, caress, pulsate and ease into morning light, sometimes alarmed at their own gymnastics but usually pleased nevertheless. Manus and Maisie got up, had breakfast together. He went to his work, she had an extra cup of tea before going to hers. Everything was natural. Just like . . . dreams. They had arranged to meet next time that Manus was in Dublin, which happily was in two days time. Two long days. Maisie thought about love and lust and wonder. She had another cup of tea.

'New man is it?' one of her housemates asked, as he popped his toast. 'Slightly uptempo from your usual anarchist?'

Maisie raised her voice slightly. 'Anarchist? In which sense do you mean, Gordon dear? You could hardly call my last two usuals anarchists. Neither of them was bright enough.'

'Perhaps I should search for another word, Maisie darling,' Gordon sniffed. Gordon felt ill when he thought of the ease with which Maisie changed her men. Of course they must be fools too but still it made a man feel uneasy. Maisie felt good. She was not going to argue even with Gordon this morning. She found no amusement in it. Usually she enjoyed him. These two could insult each other, careful to keep the barb in the voice well concealed so either of them could laugh at any given moment, as if it was all pleasant teasing. Not this morning. She wanted to be alone now to think about last night. Not really about last night but about Manus. Maeve came in and shuffled herself around the room getting breakfast. She never spoke in the mornings, which suited Maisie fine. These two spoke intimately and seriously at monthly intervals (either one of them was drunk or the other had her period) and then spent their daily encounters regaining a respectable distance, until the next time. Breakfast was always distance time, even if they were nearing their next mutual outpouring. Claire, the other house partner, was rarely there. She kept the address, maybe for appearances or maybe because of some rooted independence that didn't allow her to move *all* her belongings into the boyfriend's place. She wasn't here this morning either. Gordon finished breakfast. Maeve lapsed behind her book. What was she, Maisie, doing living with these people? There wasn't an inch of life between them. She sighed quietly but deeply and went to work. She walked, so that she would have time to think about Manus. Dublin in the morning was a great place for a walk — you looked and stepped to the sound of everyone else's thoughts; that is if you had nothing to think about yourself. This morning, Maisie never saw a word that the others were breathing or thinking.

Someone else was thinking about Manus too. She was forty-three to-day. She too had been walking. She had walked the children to school because she really did need some regular exercise. Her clothes were beginning to look puffed. All the tans in a travel brochure couldn't black out fat. It was a pity that Manus had to stay in Dublin last night but Catherine was used to that by now and he would be home this evening. They were going out to dinner to celebrate her birthday. More food.

Catherine had married Manus twenty years ago. Twenty years is a long time. She was twenty-three then. She had believed in romantic love. She had no reason not to. There were people around her who didn't seem to have that promised satisfied aura but they were only those people. They weren't her. People still cried at weddings. Cried, not sniffed. Particularly the mother of the bride. But still Catherine believed. And why not? There wasn't much else to believe. Why should she be the one to question? She had never met anyone who had, and anyway there were all those songs. Ah! Catherine. She married Manus, who was smug, even at twenty-five. He had been cushioned from pain all his life by his unimaginative mother, his sister, one first tentative girlfriend (who detested him ever since) and now Catherine. He could take all that without appearing to be getting anything. His character was full and confident even if it was based on a rather shaky foundation. They had three children, two girls and then the boy. She would have continued having more to get the son, for Manus, but luckily it came third. She then herded onto the Pill with all the rest of the women of her age for fifteen years before she read somewhere that it wasn't safe. She went off it then and felt a bit better. Manus was a good enough man. They fell out of that romantic love very soon after the second child. She wouldn't have known whether it was the children, or time, or boredom, if she'd thought about it. Which she didn't. When things were very dull they would rediscuss the night they had met and maybe the first month of their romance. This challenge never failed to rouse them both. After ten or twelve years they stopped even that. Something — disappointment, perhaps even anger — sat like a dull cloud somewhere above Catherine's stomach, but she didn't know about it. She bore grudges like overdue children. Life went on. She went the way of all good women who have families and away-a-lot husbands. Into tweed coats and fat. She was forty-three today and they were going for dinner. Something, even if it was only endurance, mut have been successful.

The next two days were long but enjoyable for both Manus and Maisie. Their pulses throbbed at the bottom of their bodies.

Thursday. They met after work. How would they

get on now, without a party or a goodly quantity of drink? They exchanged counties of origin, schools and other small pieces of background information. Their exchanges became monuments in the world of romance and passion. But they were real people too, despite the pretence at extreme civilization, and they soon hacked their way through the preliminaries to bed. Daylight shone on them as they felt and marked the lines of their lives. They tucked their feet one under each, before they slid themselves around and into each other. They broke the terrible silence of the world with whispered love words and Maisie cried involuntarily from emptiness, as they climaxed together. They lay for some minutes and now she thought to look into his eyes. She was thinking — My God, I think that I love the man. But Manus wouldn't meet her eyes. He shifted uncomfortably under her look — he knew it. Nevertheless, they met again. Several times. Soon Maisie could no longer remember days without him. But she knew something else too. Yet she was afraid to ask. By the time he told her that he was a married father she had worked herself into a cold acceptance of their situation. But still it came as a shock to her — the way he told her. The way he looked. He moved away miles, years, as he named his wife and children. It was the way he did it. Maisie could see in the gesture that he expected her to accept. There was a pain in her throat. She saw that he had never loved her, he had merely become addicted to the sex. A heavy pity for his wife settled on her. She shrugged it off. She had to think quickly. Now it was up to her. Be the second woman? Play cheat? Be fair? Never. She couldn't now.

'There's a good film on television. Gordon and Maeve are both out.' They went to bed. She thought about his wife while he made love to her, with a skill and a tenderness that he never knew he had in himself. He'd

lifted his guilt, which he didn't know he had, and placed
it firmly on Maisie's heart.

'Manus, I . . .'

'She wouldn't think of you.'

'So you say. It's in your interests to do so.'

She got up, made tea, and got him ready for home.
(Never again could she spend all night with him.) The
movements, the arrangements, the established
patterns all fitted together now in her head, as she saw
him off in his red car. Of course she'd known.

First there was the half bottle of whiskey and then
there was the bottle of cooking sherry in the cupboard.

Hours later, in the middle of the night, Maeve and
Maisie were still talking, exhausted. Maeve did her best
to get Maisie to give him up. This wasn't going to
benefit anybody. Maisie gave him up. Then cried that
she couldn't. And indeed she couldn't.

'And he doesn't love his wife. She's dead boring. Do
you know what I heard the other day? Bloody wives
sending Valentine messages to their husbands on the
radio, even though they knew that the husbands were
at work and that there was no radio at work.'

'I don't think that has anything to do with this
particular wife.'

'They're all the same.'

'Stop being so young.'

Maeve tried another tack, a hint of unblaming
sympathy for this anonymous wife. Maisie listened
with her eyes wide open, more from the drink than
comprehension or agreement.

'Women with children come to life late — at least
they come to living late, Maisie. Honestly. He probably
is still in love with his wife.'

'Do you really believe that?'

'Yes, and most of them don't ever come back to
living because they're too finished, too tired, by then.

But their husbands love them and they wait.'

'What are you talking about?'

'They know they've ruined themselves and some of them try to ruin their husbands too. Proper revenge — you know, that sort of thing.'

'Well, why the fuck do they have children then?'

Maisie was shrilling now. Maeve was still calm. After all, in the end it was only a conversation to her.

'To place themselves, and because they don't know. They think that they will live longer that way.'

'Crap.'

She got up to go to bed. Her eyes were full of tears. Her heart was mercifully like lead.

'Thank you Maeve.'

She stumbled into her room and fell on the bed, unable to get under the warm covers for even that much comfort. She didn't want to talk about children. Children came from pregnancies. She was worried. She wasn't that late but . . . But she couldn't, she couldn't be. SHE couldn't be. Of course it was possible, but no, no, she couldn't be. Manus, like every other man before, hadn't asked. You had to go abroad for that. Presumed she would have looked after those matters. That is if he thought about it at all. Maisie had gone on the wing and the prayer. He was so nice — he must know that it was all right. Perhaps he was sterile. Ah! Maisie. Go to sleep Maisie. Go to sleep. Wait a few more days. Sleep.

Maisie didn't sleep very well. She had a thumping, not a euphoric, hangover. It was Monday. Manus didn't ring all week. She couldn't ring. She had done herself and his wife the favour of not asking him for his telephone number. She slumped into hour-to-hour living, smoking forty cigarettes a day. The cigarettes in turn gave her another headache. She went to the toilet as if she was going on a pilgrimage. But the shrine produced no miracles. It was Friday. She went home, to

her real home, to Mother and Father, to Mr and Mrs
Ryan, for the weekend. She did sleep well on Friday
night. But she woke suddenly. She was either pregnant
or she wasn't. It was simple. Is, isn't. Is, isn't. Why did so
much depend on that one are, aren't. Nothing else ever
mattered so much except perhaps she's dead, she's
alive. One spot of red, glorious red, would pronounce
her alive and well. Dear god, I'll kiss my periods if I get
them. No, that wouldn't do. Dear god, I'll never do it
again. Maisie had no hope left. The past week had got
rid of all those childish dreams that make it all right, that
make every morning see a new different sunshine.
Many people, she supposed, lived with those
childlikenesses until the day they died. Not Maisie. Not
any more. She didn't even run her finger through her
sleeping hair into her warm dark dark corners to see if
there was any red blood.

She couldn't hang around her parents in their
country peace. There was so much of time here that she
might blurt out something and there was no need for
that. There would be no need for that. Them, crying,
clutching their chests as if they were having heart
attacks, was more than she could stand. Also, it was
difficult to get sick without being heard. So she went
back to her hole of a house on the dismal Saturday
evening, and drank herself asleep. Half waking at five
o'clock she understood — I will die someday. I will not be
here always. I will go because I will have to go. To go
alone. And I will be terrified. Everyone goes. They're all
little dots, with only a few years each. Floating dots.
Why all this? Why put all those dots through so much
hope, pain and history for death at the end. It wasn't
fair. Mother. Father. Manus. Me. We'll all go. Manus's
wife. We'll all go, soon. Each of us alone. Me more alone
than the rest. She woke a bit more. Sick. Sweat all over
her body. Fuck it. That's death, this is worse. People

won't blame me for dying. People are too afraid of death — they do not attach blame. When she was young long long long ago she had always wanted to ask old people if they were afraid of dying. But even then she knew something about tact. Were pregnant people afraid? Go to sleep. Try to sleep Maisie. Hope. What's wrong with hope? Dying people hope. Or do they? God no, not again. Something light. Think of something light. She must look at last month's horoscope in the morning. For the laugh. Was it Jehovah or Saint Bernadette that forecast a world war? That was easy. Did people forecast pregnancy? She would have to get up. She couldn't go back to sleep. In order to sleep during a crisis you must have either religion or drink.

Monday. Had my test. Just as I thought. That's that. No more wondering.

Maisie went to work every morning. She got sick first thing, then had toast. She didn't worry all the time — just drifted and panicked and cried and drifted. This wasn't the old terror of the dark ages. This was the new terror. More choices. Same terror. A dazed contemplative sort of fear. Maeve wanted to be sympathetic but the look in Maisie's eyes was hard to take. Nothing seemed to register.

'What are you going to do?'

Maisie looked at her.

'What about Manus?'

Maisie looked at her.

Thursday. Manus rang. We are meeting tonight.

Manus said two things. First, 'It's not mine.' Maisie looked at him, through him. She thought — how could I have sunk so low for a fuck? But it was love. Wasn't it? Second, 'I will support you in whatever you want to do. I will get you the money tomorrow.'

'What money?'

'Come on, Maisie. You're liberal. More liberal than

me.'

He managed to make it sound enviable and dirty. Manus was thinking that she was going to turn out difficult. He'd have to spend a few days with her to convince her. She'd like that. Awkward. Catherine and he and the kids were booked on a holiday. Catherine would be no problem, but changing holidays could be difficult and he certainly couldn't afford to leave this business until the holidays were over. It might be too late by then. How unfortunate it had to happen at this precise time. He decided against suggesting that they sleep together although really he should have, considering that she certainly couldn't get pregnant out of it.

Maeve and Maisie talked endlessly but nothing new came through their weary repeated sentences until one evening Maeve came home excited beyond imagination, for her. She had overheard a conversation between Manus and a lanky cocksure loud creep. Actually he wasn't that loud but when Maeve saw Manus she had sidled into the next booth in the restaurant and put her ears out on stalks.

Loud cocksure creep: 'How do you think you'll do next time?'

Manus: 'I presume I'll get a few thousand more than the last time.'

Loud cocksure creep: 'You should old chap, you should. A pregnant wife never harmed a sitting member. (Loud laughter.) Any TD going for his second turn around finds that it's a help, actually. Good family man, all that stuff. When's your wife due?'

Maeve concentrated on the lettuce on her plate. If she moved she might vomit. But she was no dozer. She saw possibilities. Not just for Maisie — money and all that. Not really bribery — but for herself too. Excitement. Journalists maybe. After the money.

Maisie deserved something cheerful. She rushed home and repeated the conversation to Maisie, except for the pregnant wife bit. Maisie looked at her. Maeve, who knew no better, felt her patience wearing thin with this pregnant state.

'Do you hear me? A TD, I said. A Teachta Dawla. A member of the Dáil, dear. The Dáil. The parliament of this here country. Think of what this means!'

Maisie was tired.

'I don't give two tuppenny fucks what he is. It makes no difference to me what his sperm bank was attached to or what it does for a living. No difference at all. Pregnant is pregnant.'

She was only slightly hurt that he had told her another lie. What was one more? Maeve was fuming at this obvious stupidity.

'A TD. Let me tell you . . .'

'No let me tell you. He can be a computer person in IC, a travelling salesman, he can be nothing . . . it makes no difference to me. No difference *at all*, is that clear?'

'OK, OK. If that's the way you want it. But I wasn't talking just about you being pregnant . . .'

Maisie was staring at her.

'. . . about how you got pregnant, I mean. I was . . .'

'I'm going to be sick . . .'

Maisie took the money. The exact amount, no more no less. He must have worked out the price of the tea on the boat over. She got it by post. Made to order, unsigned. No cheque book stubs to be found. Manus was no fool. She decided to have it — the baby, not the abortion — in England. Easier all round that way, for everyone else. She would have to leave the house even if she did stay in Dublin. Maeve had become less sympathetic since the TD nonsense. Gordon was shocked, really. His imagination about these matters got bogged down quickly, but a person like Maisie pregnant! All those perfectly lovely women who couldn't have babies ... Her as a mother didn't bear thinking about. That will teach her. Bet she doesn't know who the father is. Men should be more careful. You wouldn't want just anyone rearing your child.

Before Maisie ran away from Dublin she rang the clinic of Manus O'Brien.

'Sorry for bothering you, Miss. I'm doing a survey on attitudinal changes in Ireland. I was wondering if you could tell me where Mr O'Brien stands on the abortion issue?

'Miss, whatever your name is — Mr O'Brien is naturally opposed to abortion.'

'Naturally. I thought as much. Thank you, Miss.'

'Mrs. Mrs O'Brien.'

'I see. Thank you Mrs O'Brien. Very nice to talk to you. Thank you for your help.'

Maisie felt a moment of sympathy for the other woman. She wished that she could see her, just once, in some crowded place, so she could nod sympathetically in her direction.

Eight and a half months later. Dear Mother and Father. I am sorry that I broke your hearts. I have given birth to a lovely baby girl. I am sorry that I got pregnant and that I could not talk to you about it. I remain your loving daughter, Maisie. Dear Maeve. I am sorry for leaving so quickly but I was too confused to stay. I know that you think it was cowardly but I actually felt brave. Funny that. I've had a lovely daughter. I cried for all of you and for me and for her when she was born. Sorry about the sloppiness. I'm utterly lonely. Your friend Maisie.

Sorry. Sorry. Sorry.

Fuck that. Manus O'Brien TD Stop A daughter was born to you this month Stop Actually it was born to me Stop The money came in handy Stop

Manus, with a red face and a turkey-coloured neck, flustered to his secretary that his brother was playing a practical joke on him. 'Actually,' he said, making a great attempt to cover up (The bitch. The bitch. He'd never have a minute's peace from now on. I wonder what blood group was the bastard?) 'I'm expecting another son.'

Maisie registered her daughter. She was now responsible, twenty-three, and learned. She had become a silent citizen, a fool. No. No, not that. A silenced citizen, away, with a destroyed life and name. A freed person — there was nothing left to lose. Ah! such a wise wise woman.

The Letter

The bedclothes were heavy on Sarah. She was flattened on the boards already and the clothes pushed her down even further, if that was possible. She turned on her side and wrapped her legs up by hugging her knees, which were much too jagged to give any warmth or solid comfort. There was nothing warm in this room. She tried not to look. It was as if they brought you to a mental hospital then tried to stop you feeling warm again. Perhaps if you could get warm you'd be happy here and would make no effort.

Mental? Of course she was mental. Anyone with brains was mental. How could they not be? The mental mind. Some brainy people had more control than others. She had controlled for a long time, no matter what happened, no matter what some idiot said, no matter how they ignored her. Her body began to take on peculiar shapes from the effort of restraining herself. But then she started thinking in the evenings, something to do with her periods or her life, and didn't see why she should control herself, it, any more. They brought her here then after she tried to kill herself. Sarah did feel better now than she had that particular evening. She had to admit that. But today, she was cold and was sorry that she hadn't succeeded — such a blatant insult to the gift of life. Sarah was in love with thoughts like that. Now all that any of these people or her relatives thought was that she had been handing around a cry for help like some love-desperate youngster. You bet they were going to watch her. She supposed she did need some help but they couldn't give it to her so what was the point of them jibbering over her in words that they didn't understand? Or peering at her. Did they want to keep her alive so that they could prove to each other that they had helped her? If only they could see the clarity of that moment. All the despair that led her there had been worth it just for that flash of certainty. No point now in thinking about it. She would court death again if ever she felt that passion, but that might be never.

Now that she thought about it, all her life had been leading to this. No surprise at all. She had been a cranky, wise child. She had been bright at school, not given to extremes, but noticeably partial to day-dreaming — 'A vivid imagination which helps her with her essays.' Just like them. That was all they could ever do. Find a function for your very being. From there she had gone on to do the normal things. She had gone to university but couldn't stick it. The place was full of insipid rich. She had got married, had children, and gone mad.

The doctor came. Sarah looked at his head. It was an even, oval shape — his mother would have had an easy delivery. He looked pleasant enough — really. Was probably a good child. How did they gather all that obnoxious confidence about themselves? Another doctor came. His hands were cold. 'Now Sarah, we' (he was on his own) 'just want to ask you a few questions, just to check the old brain, you know.' Perhaps he hadn't said 'the old brain', but Sarah knew what he meant. 'What are the names of your children?' Oh Jesus Christ she moaned, surely they don't think that I've forgotten them. Another doctor came hurrying staidly to her bed. I may have cheated them or was it cheating? I couldn't help knowing what I know. Is the babysitter being diplomatic?

'What are your children's names, Sarah. Surely you must remember?'

'Of course I bloody remember. I had them, didn't I??? I named them, didn't I?? What do you think I am??? I am a mother you know. A M-O-T-H-E-R.'

The two doctors jumped. Nurses came running from every corner of the ward. Doesn't take much to make them run. They all looked disappointed and hurt. Sarah apologized. The doctors relaxed a little. That's the sort of thing — an apology — that goes down well when you're trying to prove how unmental you are. It was going to be terribly hard to convince them, all the same. She would have to though, so that she could get out to get on with clocking in the days until some disease wiped her out. And to get warm. It's funny how they never held it against you if you put yourself in the way of some disease and died slowly. They could be self-righteous about disease. It was the suddenness of suicide that unnerved them. Maybe she'd go to some country that was riddled with disease. And warm on top of it.

'What ages are they?'

'Four and two'. Nice and even.

'And how are you feeling yourself today? You're not depressed are you?'

'Oh, no. Not at all. I'm feeling great. Great, thank you.'

That was well done.

I was in the air poised between a life of service and the ease of a warm coffin. What do you want me to do? Cover my body, make breakfast, talk nice, complain seldom, accept dictionary meanings of words. Who wrote those meaningless dictionaries? No, it would never do to say that.

The doctors moved to the next bed. The nurses faded back to the corners of their wards. This woman, in the next bed, had gone crazy, according to the neighbours, after her sixth child. They couldn't understand why because she was delighted about the baby, although mind you they themselves thought that six was a bit much. Would they ask her the names of all six or just the five? Sarah pulled the clothes around her ears. That night she dreamt of strange hands. Some had blue cold knuckles. Others were purple, greasy, fat. One moved rhythmically over, in circles, stylishly around and then went off in the clouds.

Some weeks later Sarah went home. She clutched the bedclothes every night and she sometimes had a funny look about her, but all in all the doctors were pleased with the extent of her recovery. Her family were pleased more with the speed than the extent of her return to normality. In no time at all no one would remember the whole sordid business. When they called now, the house was always neat. The children never had a run in their noses. Sarah spun round on the continual test. She hoovered the corners of the stairs. She had never thought of that place before. She boiled the tea cloths — more cleanliness. She dusted the sitting room three or four times a week. She did a never-ending round of shopping so the fridge would always be full. She bathed the children every night, brushed their hair, bought them endless toothbrushes, kept their nails trim, and re-dressed them in clean clothes perhaps three times a day. Who is mental now?

Her family were right. Soon the whole terrible episode was forgotten or apparently so, although you could never be sure of neighbours. Sarah lived and brought her children up. She died young as a result of cancer, a disease she picked up in her dreams at night.

The morning she died the house was spotless and the children nearly reared, thank God for that anyway. She left a long startling letter. It had individual messages for a lot of people. Who would have thought that Sarah was so bright in spots? Or that she was thinking things like that? Some of her jabs were very near the bone, but of course she had never really got over that time she went mental. The trouble about all the messages being in the one letter was that when Rose was given the letter to read her message she also read all the others. As did May and John and every one of them. Made you feel small.

The Pattern

Mr Roche was extremely surprised by the note on his desk. He had arrived at the office slightly late which was very unlike him. Often the receptionist would have delivered his post in the tray before he arrived. He had managed to train her well, he mused to himself. She didn't even know what a letter opener was when she came to work for him. Now she efficiently slit his letters open each morning and piled them neatly on the left-hand side of his phone, usually dusting the phone at the same time. It had been quite a task, training this particular young lady, Mr Roche reckoned. She had been an over-bright flushed sort of girl who exuded much too much vitality for a quiet office like his. In her first week she had engaged in rather deep conversations — the sort that might extend beyond the cafeteria — and she had shown a marked reluctance to buckle under and learn how to be a proper receptionist. It was as if she didn't want to learn, as if she thought that she was somehow above it. But the right measure of minor humiliation, aloofness and mature half smiles — quickly followed by brisk orders — had eventually paid off. She was now all he could wish for and whatever high falutin notions she had previously nurtured about herself were now gone, or at least were hidden well enough not to be a source of disruption. This morning, she had not delivered his letters but instead had propped a neat memo against his phone. He looked at it again. It definitely read 'Miss Smyth rang. She did not want to leave any message.' He couldn't believe this memo. What on earth had Miss Smyth been ringing for? Perhaps it was a Mr Smyth. But no ..., the receptionist didn't make mistakes like that any more. Miss Smyth had obviously telephoned. But why?

Mr Roche wondered for some time, tossed around some possibilities and then decided to forget it. He had a lot of work to do today. He had been delegated to meet some members of the union, a task he detested. Union members were so predictable, so earnest, so boring ... this part of business he hated. He really only wished to mix with his peers. Sitting around trying to make small talk with his lessers didn't impress him at all. He wondered though, did they find him more convivial than the other managers? He doubted if the others deliberately made efforts to lower themselves to the appropriate level. He had no idea at all that in union circles he was considered decidedly simple. The phone rang. Mr Roche started slightly. But it was only Davis & Blennerhassett inquiring about import duty on razor blades. He sighed. If it was anything serious Miss Smyth would ring back. Of course. No need to fluster any more. It was good that he'd thought of that before wasting any more time.

The morning stuttered on nervously. Mr Roche was agitated. On several occasions he lifted the phone intending to get the receptionist to put him through to Miss Smyth. But then no. He put it down each time. This was preposterous. Mr Roche was not used to being undecided and time was being wasted as well. He went for morning coffee. He drank his usual half cup and ate his arrowroot biscuit, wishing all the time that he could dunk it. He always wanted to do this when he was disturbed. He supposed that none of his staff ever thought of his small human needs. Pity really. When he left the table early someone remarked that Mr Roche seemed strange this morning. 'Not a bit more than usual,' sniffed one young clerk — the clerk that everyone (well everyone who mattered) agreed was a cheeky young brat. Every time redundancy was mentioned people thought of her. He went back to his office, told the receptionist not to disturb him and tried to work out what to do. He'd better do something or he'd get no work done. The truth of the matter was — he doodled excessively — he had known (if known was a strong enough word) Miss Smyth for six years and never ever in all that time had she — or he for that matter — done anything unpredictable. Nothing that was, until this phone call today. Yes, there had been a few heady days in the first month, but then things settled down and all had been well since. Six years was a long time and he was upset at this emergence of the unusual. The crux of the matter was that a rigid satisfactory pattern was the basis of their friendship. The pattern depended on regular, not too regular, contact. They rang each other every alternate fortnight and it wasn't her turn. She had broken the pattern. He couldn't believe that she would do anything to jeopardize their little whatever-you'd-call-it, but there you are, she had. It was most upsetting. He checked the calendar, not that there was any need, and yes she had rung thirteen days ago. Strange. Really strange.

Mr Roche sighed and decided to put the whole thing out of his mind. He tried to catch up on his work. Damn it — he started wondering again. Had some close relation or friend of Miss Smyth's died? Was she perhaps changing her accommodation — or her job? No. Never her job. She had a good job. In fact, Mr Roche often thought that she was very lucky to have the job that she had. Her education had finished early, much to her grief, and she had spent fifteen years in and out of various jobs, each one slightly better than the last one in some respects, and slightly worse in others — worse usually in the trivial ways that made those jobs bearable. When she finally landed this job there was a dramatic rather than minor change. Within a few months she was trusted with the innermost secrets of Preston Ltd and was elevated to position of assistant manager in every way except name — and pay of course. She bought and sold for Preston Ltd. She presented them, represented them and praised them highly. No, she would never leave that job for indeed she was lucky — a woman with her meagre qualifications. True, she had wit and dreams that had no place in Preston Ltd during the day and little chance of flourishing in the tired evenings, but she couldn't expect everything. Indeed Miss Smyth had often told Mr Roche that she couldn't want for better — although she confided in him on one of those rare evenings when near-intimate details were exchanged, that as a child she had wanted to do two things with her life — learn opera singing and become a professional gardener. 'Really,' replied Mr Roche, frightened actually at the prospect that she might have done either. Opera singing maybe — actually, come to think of it — that might have been interesting. Having a friendship with an opera singer? Still, *no*. She would have been different. More self-opinionated, he supposed and really she was sufficiently self-assured as it *was*. Gardening! Can you imagine? He looked at her and she had a dreamy dangerous sort of look in her eyes. Clouded. Yes, her eyes were clouded. He felt like patting her on the head, or maybe the shoulder, but in their circumstances it wouldn't be right. So he coughed and changed the subject. He made a mental note to stick to theatre rather than pubs.

But that was a long time ago. Now here he was trying unsuccessfully to get through a day's work. Then it struck him — of course — of course — she had forgotten. She had forgotten that it was his turn to ring. That was it. She hadn't simply decided to break the routine. It was merely understandable human error on her part. Wasn't it amazing that he hadn't thought of that before! This of course was what happened when well-established patterns were upset — one got so worried one couldn't think of the most obvious of things. The whole morning was nearly gone. And she had just forgotten. He decided against lunch because what with the phone call and the union matter he hadn't got settled into the estimates at all. This turned out to be a bad idea. Lunch talk with the other managers would have helped him to concentrate on these damned endless figures. As it was he was making no progress because thoughts of his long knowledge of Miss Smyth kept drifting over him, making him nervous and agitated.

They had met at the Era Berk Christmas party six years ago. Miss Smyth was there representing Preston Ltd. He had attended just to put in an appearance for his firm. It was the usual Christmas gathering. Young spivs who couldn't drink, drinking too much and slobbering on to embarrassed (or delighted, as the case may be) sober middle management. Miss Smyth and Mr Roche introduced themselves when they arrived at the same floor position at the same time. A bit like life really, he thought. They were both alone at the party. Otherwise they wouldn't have behaved as they did. They went home together after having spent a pleasant evening chatting and, as Mr Roche realised later, drinking too much. They had coffee. An indiscretion followed. However, before they parted Miss Smyth and Mr Roche assured each other that this was not their normal behaviour.

In the following weeks both reacted quite differently to the night's caper. Mr Roche blushed frequently and would have said 'Geee Zuss — I die every time I think of it,' if he had only known how. However, not having any experience or language to get him through this embarrassing time, he simply waited, knowing that like everything difficult it would pass with time. And indeed the acute shivering that accompanied each memory-burst disappeared completely, when it began to dawn on him that Miss Smyth had in fact initiated whatever had gone on between them. Now as far as he could remember, that's what had happened.

Miss Smyth, on the other hand, viewed the evening rather more maturely. She woke in such good form the next day that she decided, without the usual hesitation, to visit her married younger sister, who had four children. She normally had to force herself to make the journey, not that she didn't like her sister, but frankly because she didn't like children. She had also told her sister that she had never, even for a moment, contemplated marriage. Therefore the two sisters got along well. They each felt sorry for the other but were happy in each other's company, despite the fact that brute honesty could have upset the balance on many an occasion.

'Auntie Annie, Auntie Annie,' they chorused. 'Auntie Annie's here.' If they must put a tag on her she wished it could be Aunt. 'Anne, great you're here. God you look well. Dare I, dare I ask you to babysit?' 'Of course.' And so Anne Smyth never got to share her little joy with her sister that evening. Next time she called she had decided to keep it to herself because she had discovered how much she enjoyed private recollection of the Era Berk Christmas party. She did occasionally wonder if she should expect more, but for the moment she felt content with the startling tight currents that caroused through her body and with the memory of bold candid words, spoken with the dignity due to her age. Anne Smyth was happy.

Some time later Mr Roche rang Miss Smyth. Having recovered from all the after effects and having cleared his mind of the complications of guilt, he thought it would be a nice gesture. He didn't want her to think that he was unduly shocked at her forwardness and he had, after all, enjoyed her company. They arranged to go for a meal. Afterwards they went to their respective homes. He was happy. She was put out at the abrupt end to the evening but the presence of Mr Roche had reawakened the bodily joys within her so she wasn't completely disappointed. Two weeks later Anne Smyth rang Mr Roche. She simply didn't see why she shouldn't. She offered to treat him to dinner, careful to suggest by the tone of her voice, two options as to her reasons — either she was grateful for his companionship or she wished to develop their friendship into something more appropriate to their age. He chose the first option. And she acquiesed, because it was better to have fodder for her dreams than have no dreams at all. And so the pattern started. Started because Mr Roche felt that it was necessary, so that two people could withdraw from what he saw as an unfortunate intimacy. An intimacy caused by drink. Thereafter they met every fortnight. They went to the theatre regularly. They went for meals and very rarely for a drink. They also went to the cinema — if there was something really good on, which of course wasn't very often. They both thought that mediocre theatre was bearable — mediocre cinema inexcusable. The advantage of the pattern, apart from the obvious (to Mr Roche, that is) was that a certain type of dependability without demand was established. As far as Mr Roche could remember, credit for this solid arrangement, advantageous naturally to both, for surely Miss Smyth wanted order in her life, rested with himself. Another advantage was that one didn't waste time thinking about unexpected phone calls — at least one Mr Roche didn't. He shuddered at the thought of other days like this. Five o'clock came. All that dreaming. All those unfinished schedules. He was a purple shade of resentful at Miss Smyth. And he would have to come in early in the morning. Funny. If there was something serious up she hadn't rung back. But no — she had simply forgotten and in the circumstances, for both their sakes, he thought it best not to return the call. He left the office. The receptionist had left early. He went home, drained and exhausted.

Anne Smyth had in fact often thought of ringing Mr Roche out of turn. Often. She had thought things like 'Mr Roche, you're in for a land this morning cherub,' or 'By Jesus I'll muck you up proper today yet,' or ''Morning Tootsie Wootsie.' But she was lonely too and didn't want to give up the thread of normality that linked her with other people — dates. So she hadn't ever rung out of turn. Neither had she rung this morning. It was 'Miss Smyth's office,' that rang with 'an urgent message for a Mr Roche.'

The receptionist was afraid to tell Mr Roche so she left early in order to give him a chance to get the bad news in private. The receptionist and the cheeky clerk were in fact great drinking pals of Anne Smyth's so they knew the whole story. But Mr Roche went home without returning the call and the office didn't like to be over presumptuous by ringing again. Presumably he found out in a fortnight when he made his due call. A fortnight, yes, because the whole pattern was upset now anyway.

The Day
She Lost
the Last of
Her Friends

It was 2035 or 1935 in Ireland, depending on your humour. Elsewhere it was uniformly 1985. In Ireland they had damned every woman for her womb. For having children, for not having children. For dying giving birth, for not dying giving birth. Into this morning, stepped Rose. Gingerly. They called her separated. Separated from what? She felt intact. Except for one thing. She had a lot of problems with her friends. She had children. This didn't help. They hadn't, or if they had they were organized, married and had money. Her friends were a strange combination. Some of them couldn't be allowed to meet others of them. But they got her through, and she gave as much blinkered uninformed loyalty as she got, she was sure.

As far as friendships went her mother had, two decades ago, been satisfied that she was normal.

She had lost a combination of minor friends when she started natalizing. They'd fallen off for their own peculiar reasons as the first child got its first tooth, after weeks of dribbling and screaming, as she fought her corner not to have the second baptized while they cooed, 'The poor child, the poor pagan, it will feel left out, it will have problems later on,' or as she moved her Indian tea-sets, her red-pencilled maps of Asia, her wall coverings, her discarded photo albums, into the unwelcoming house in the suburbs. The good flat was too small after the third. She never worried about them. This was everyone's life. Then a large slice of the friendship pile moved off with the husband when he left. Why wouldn't they? He had a job, needed sympathy, and wasn't half as stroppy as she. She didn't worry about them either. Who wanted fogeys like that for friends when her life was going to change completely now! Thank Christ. New people would come. They did. And gradually went. Which was hard.

First there was Mary, Anne, Maura. Then Cassie, Brendan. Mary wanted another mother. Nothing more, nothing less. Rose was cooking for four, so why not five? Anne lived in the pub. She wouldn't meet anyone anywhere else. It became tedious — conversation suspended until the alcohol level was high enough to allow honesty, always with the excuse to hand, 'God I was awful drunk last night. I hadn't eaten a proper tea. I can't remember a thing I said.' But she was the antidote to Rose's day, so Rose stayed. Eventually Anne moved on to better company. She had milked Rose for every funny child story going. She was tired of the tortured children stories. Maura needed someone to theatre-go. The times didn't suit. Cassie cooled the friendship — too intense. Never mind, Rose. Your children will grow up and you will have a wonderful wisdom, even more than you have now. Won't you be marvellous company! Everyone will want to spend an evening at your feet, hanging onto every word you say, listening to your anecdotes, hoping for a brush of your knowledge, writing down your advice for rearing children — aged two to twenty — which is, After All, the most important job in the world, they all agree. They will interview you on the radio, even. Your mother says that no one is interested in her now that she's eighty-two, but she must be wrong. She must be doting. Old women can be crabby.

Was Rose fooling herself? Was she perhaps arrogant in her survival?

Rose got very close to Mark and Nuala. When she met them first she was down on couples but this one grew on her. In the beginning he had a sheepish look when in mixed company. He'd obviously wronged Nuala recently. For Nuala's part, she wasn't comfortable with that nervous power over someone that had only got to do with guilt. Later she wronged him and they became equal out of misdeeds. Two wrongs ... Who said? He began to look less sheepish. She relaxed. Rose liked them for several reasons, their easiness mostly. They didn't treat her endlessly as a mother. They didn't need to wage that kind of power in order to have justification for being. Yet they talked to her children — talked. They didn't pat them on the head and tell their mother how lovely they were. When she met them in bars (Rose got out two nights a week one hour before closing time. That was one pint, one pound twenty — unless, unless someone offered — no forced — her to have another.) they didn't ask her in that threatening voice of other people, 'Who is babysitting?'

That was always a teller. Rose would cringe. That question was not concerned with the health or the well-being of her or anyone else's children. It was numbering her for guilt.

'You are out and some poor unfortunate is minding your children.'

'Nice of Marie to let you out.'

'Out again — mothers these days!'

But gradually — it took a year — Mark and Nuala got uneasy with her. She didn't blame them. They would be settling to do the normal things of comfortable sets of twos and in she would barge. One evening she went to their flat — she couldn't stand the loneliness, the children. Mark and Nuala had the look of two who had been disturbed at one of the delicate moments in life. She knew. But God it *was* evening. It was only evening. She stood on the doorstep, watched by her charges, who knew that their infallible mother had made some social mistake. She scurried from the door leaving some incomprehensible sentence hanging in the air. She pointed the children straight ahead and bit her lip hard, to match the pain with the other pain as the tears came to her eyes. Chin up Rose, you must, must make yourself not call so often. Dearest Rose, why are you out in the jungle when everyone else moves steadily homeward each evening? Never mind. She put the children to bed. That used up an hour. She read bits of a book looking out the window sometimes, lining up the window-ledge with the neighbour's garden wall by closing one eye and moving her head in interesting-looking directions. Curious gestures. Sometimes she blocked out all of the neighbour's wall. If you had been looking at her from a distance or on a *What's my Line* programme, you would have had great difficulty placing her.

Week 48 on the eggs started off badly. She'd had a lonely weekend. On Sunday Sadie had collected her in the spanking new car, plastic paper still intact. Sadie had been around for a year or so, not always to Rose's delight. She, Sadie, knew that she was doing a favour so she looked smart. Piety always glowed on her like new sunburn. But at least she was consistent. Rose didn't mind much about her failings and if she did she said little. Rose was motivated by a desperate need to be eternally frank so she congratulated herself for remaining silent on topics that others would not have ever dreamt of raising. Rose wanted to sort the tragedies out on the spot but others found this openness a trifle off-putting. Others simmered quietly, distanced themselves and got perspective, so they never got as hurt as Rose. Poor Rose. Did she expect too much? On the way home from this patronizing mountain jaunt a problem arose. Actually this woman was getting on Rose's nerves. Who in their right mind would take children on a car ride on a hot stuffy day like this? But who was Rose to complain. She was tired. The children were tired. They were looking at her accusingly, and could you blame them? If their mother wouldn't protect them from days like this, who would? What's that smell? The baby had shat all over the back seat. Rose moaned, tears in her voice. Sadie said, 'It's all right,' But the way she said, 'It's all right.' What she really meant was 'It's not your fault, of course, but couldn't you have controlled his bowels until we got the last two miles?' (Children always do it at the last minute.) Rose stared at her, aghast. She'd had enough of this fucking nonsense. If Sadie didn't want to have anything to do with children why was she taking *her* out for the day? She had fucking three children and Sadie knew that before she collected her today to go on this stupid drive up a few mountains, that weren't mountains at all. Snap. Rose jumped from the car pulling all three with her.

'Fuck your car, your boyfriend, your bloody job. You wouldn't be here anyway only that he's gone to see his fucking mother.' She slammed the door and for effect the gods were with her. The window smashed into smithereens.

'Stop being so fucking pious. Maybe you should have stayed way back where you were when I met you. Look what you've learned from me. Sadie baby, you'll have the benefits some day of knowing me.'

Good girl Rosie. Was she perhaps a little over-confident? She headed home with the children, pointing herself and them due west.

'And another thing. Fuck your plastic covers. We're not incontinent.'

'Mammy, why are we walking?'

'Because, dear, we're all cramped up in that little car.'

'Mammy . . . Mammy . . . Mammy . . . Mammy . . .'

Rose laughed out loud. At last.

'I'd say that's that, wouldn't you?'

'What did you say, Mammy?'

They got home eventually. Years later she would forget their sore little feet, their cries, her guilt. She put them to bed.

Then there was Declan. He had the wrong name. He was wearing Rose's youngest strapped to his front, delighted with himself and with the warmth that was coming from the baby. Rose was walking beside him, thinking — Men need that, they get so little of it elsewhere and they're not allowed to let on if they need it. The only time they're allowed to coo is for two to three days after their own women have children. No wonder some of them want ten children — that's still only thirty days' cooing.

There he was, this man, Rose's friend, beaming his way down Grafton Street, warm all over with the sheer pleasure of it, when one of his cronies, (silk suit, baby-faced from too good care and food, intelligence limited, limited, zilch type) jumped out at him from the corner of South Anne Street and sneered at him.

'Is this your own?'

There was a lot to that remark. A real dig. Could

men who want to carry babies have spunk? Rose's friend was shattered. She jumped to his rescue.

'Men don't have children, dear.'

The limited intelligence bloke withered. Something about the way she said that. He walked away, getting vicious for the next woman. Declan left the island. There was no country for him.

Who was left? Charlie was gone back to jail. Lovely kind Charlie. She still wrote him letters. He wrote back. But he was lost to the world. For a long time to come. She couldn't very well write, 'Dear Charlie, I'm lonely . . .'

Can you imagine?

'Dear Rose, Go fuck yourself and count your blessings.'

No. She looked out the window. The children were asleep. 'I'll be proved right in the end by history,' she said to herself. Right about what?

She had a dream that night that friends dropped from the sky, from the roof, came through the walls shouting.

'Please Rose, go take a break. What with our lifestyles we don't get time to light fires and we also need contact with children. Your children, specifically. For a month.'

That sort of dream. She woke questioning, 'Is this dancing day for the oldest?' and then remembered that they all had the measles and that she'd been up half the night. She laughed. So all, even this, comes down to humour. How else?

The night she went to bed with Vincent (you see, things always do improve) she couldn't believe that it was happening. Now she knew that she had fancied him for a long time but never dared to think it. The sex was difficult because they were shy, she because she liked him so much and because he was a highly strung enigma, one minute funny the next deadly nervous; he

..., he didn't know why. But she woke feeling pleasant. It had been good talking, too. She didn't often feel that. It was hard saying goodbye because they were attempting to be laid back, and who was going to say 'When will I see you again?' In the end she stammered it out and went red. He didn't really answer her. Oh! Jesus he didn't want to. Once he left she thought about pain being political. She didn't want much to think that sex was. She was sad now that she knew for certain that they wouldn't be doing that again and she knew that it had something to do with the kids. He had never relaxed after she had shot out of the bed, to prevent them from seeing him. Perhaps listening to her being a mother had put him off? That wasn't courteous of him. He should have known that she had to do that, because narrower people might tell her children that she was wrong. Which she wasn't.

Ah! Rose. If you could make up the world again so that you could live in it. Fuck him. She had asked all the questions, anyway. Not just the how-many-brothers-and-sisters-do-you-have ones, but the how-did-your-mother's-death-affect-you ones as well. He hadn't asked her anything and there was a lot to know. To hell with him. Ah! but she liked him. She wasn't supposed to tell anyone about their little evening, as he called it, but some divilment caught her the next time she bumped into him publicly, surrounded by his business friends, and looking a lot different than she had seen him looking. She introduced her youngest child, who wouldn't mind being used, 'Have you met Vincent?' Vincent shifted uneasily. Loudly she said to the child, 'Get to know him, because if I have anything to do with it you'll be meeting him again, some morning over breakfast.'

That did it. That put paid to any chance that she might have had. He stared through her from a thousand miles away. Fuck him, she thought, he's bloody gorgeous.

Week 16 on the eggs the following year was dreadful. Tuesday evening snapped. She slapped her son right across the face. She stung her own hand, then cried bitterly with sorrow as she threw her arms around him trying to hold him to her, trying to apologize, to comfort, as he pulled away determined to hate her. She let him go. He ran upstairs abusing her, his little face red from her hand and dirty from vicious tears that were running into his mouth. She cried downstairs. Hopelessly. It was her friends really. If only they'd help a bit. Why should they? They hadn't made her mistakes. Still, still. You can't say you're political and not be political. Was she unreasonable? She didn't think so. That night she tucked her children in with special care. She wrote letters resigning from her various friendships and hand-delivered them in the middle of the night. She dropped a letter into her mother's letterbox telling her to get around there quick to those grandchildren of hers because their mother was going for a day or so. It was a day or so, or the mental.

She bought a one-day-return free-bottle-of-whiskey trip to Holyhead. Water would give her the notion of freedom. On the way over she flirted mildly with some men who were ultimately as sad as she. They were looking for her body. This she knew. Her body was looking too, but not for them. She needed some exoticism, not more pooling of sadness. On the way back, because time was running out, she settled for a twenty-stone Welshman who farted. They made love in a single bunk. He said that it made him realize that he needed to lose weight. She talked to herself. Rose dear, what are you doing here? But she didn't care about anything on that bunk. She enjoyed herself as the sea notched up the miles and brought them nearer to shore.

Next day she hated herself, but she couldn't figure out why. Why should she? A week later she'd forgotten the Welshman, but she still wasn't talking to any of her friends.

Elegy of Pairs

Most people in the foyer were busy at being impersonal. Dozens of others clustered together, wearing Aran sweaters and talking loudly in acquired thirty-year-old white American accents, about how they'd finally tracked down Mary's youngest, who is married to a doctor. Nice man too. He's in the Longford County. The rest of the clientele was trying hard to be stylish — to ignore these embarrassing voices. The regulars were forced by innate guilt — something they'd heard about compulsory emigration — to accept that these old fogeys had a right to come pilgriming and if they did they had to stay somewhere. Rather someplace else, but tonight there was a busload of them here. They could be ignored. The set rushed about doing just that, with the confidence of those who belong to some or other inner circle.

Chris walked in. She saw the type of place it was and moaned. She hated the silent confident ones as much as the unfortunate loudmouths. She shouldn't have come to this reunion. But it was the reunion she came for, not the hotel. She was here now. Not much point in having got two buses just to leave again without speaking to anyone. She tried sauntering to the desk but her feet speeded up, running ahead of her body, causing some people to glance warily at her. All the others must have cars. That would account for the choice of hotel. (There was a car-park underneath.) Or someone wanted to impress with her knowledge of eating haunts. That would be Concepta Gallagher. Ah! The desk. Yes the desk. Now.

'Excuse me. Do you know where the St Francis of Assisi girls .. eh .. women .. past pupils are sitting?' Why hadn't someone left a name? Probably hadn't a name of their own between them by now ... Fools ..

'Yes indeed, Madam. Come this way.'

Madam covers either Miss or Mrs and gets over Ms ... It leaves the usher in an unembarrassed position in relation to the marital status or the political opinions of the female who is looking for directions.

'This way, Madam,' through the hallway, past more grey suits, into the cocktail bar.

'Oh, they must have started their meal, Madam,' into the dining room that was suitably lit in the interests of executive discretion and deceit.

'There you are Madam.'

Indeed she was and there indeed were they, at that table over there. That was them. Poised as ever and nearly cosy. The people who never had unanswered questions. The people who never had questions, indeed. 'Here's Chris,' they sang in unison, the dreadful chorus of their schooldays unchanged. They did a reshuffle to make way for her and to distract from any awkwardness at her arrival. They settled at table again. After a few uncomfortable minutes during which they looked her over, she felt as easy with them as she'd ever felt. Food was ordered and came. They ate, and sipped the expensive wine, with the ease of those who were reared on too much. Chris, on the other hand, tasted every mouthful. They talked about what they were doing, where they were now living, who they had bumped into recently ... Chris half listened as she watched the other tables. As always she despaired. How did anyone manage to look so beautiful, so finished. They must have been born like that. Back to her own table. They exchanged expectations about summer holidays. Not still. The boarders had always spent endless hours on summer past and summer to come. No one could ever check the stories due to the distance — geographical that is — between their respective homes. Even the sound of Galway had conjured up pure magic for Chris. Josh had always thought that Chris was unsentimental — at least that's what he said. Had said. These people wouldn't know what unsentimental meant. Sentimental yes, but not unsentimental. Why was she thinking about him now? Here, of all places? There was an uneasiness about the silence at table. Someone had asked her a question. They were looking at her, waiting, What was she doing with herself?

'Something exciting no doubt.'

This with that slight twingy sound that lies uncomfortably between superiority and fear that the asker might, just might, be missing out on something.

'Who? Me? Oh, eh ... nothing much really. At the moment? I'm painting my flat and doing drama classes.'

'Painting your flat? Aren't you great! Of course you were always handy with your hands.'

Sneer. Sneer. Sneer.

Paula was sitting opposite her. Concentrate on Paula. Poor Paula. The daughter of a rich important man up in Dublin. But she always looked like a peasant, without any of the health or the droll secrecy. Perhaps it was her mother's fault? Why did she try so hard? If she left herself alone she could be real. Maybe. Chris had forgotten Paula. Completely forgotten her. No wonder. And there was Susan. She certainly looked as if she'd got where she was heading. She had been going to there, to wherever people like her head, even in the days of her grey uniform. Anne. She'd forgotten Anne too. She shouldn't have forgotten her. She was the only one who had reached for something resembling adulthood. Josh would have liked her. Did he go out on Thursday nights now? The talk was going on and on and on.

Had Chris said anything? Some drinks later she left. They pretended to believe that she was as sorry to go as she said.

The first bus was late. She and Josh had had some good times, though. And there was always that homely feeling of someone else in the house. The bus came but there were no seats unoccupied. She stood clinging to the bar as the bus driver sped dangerously and the passengers moaned, threatened, then one by one slid off in cowed silence, saying 'Thanks'. She and Josh used to have a poster over the fridge. 'Let there be Peace. At least between you and me.' Corny bloody relic of the last decade. What would the St Francis of Assissi ladies have thought of that? 'Nice,' they would have chorused. But blast it, she had thought that it was truly nice one time too, even if she did get unnerved by it during the rows.

In the end she and Josh had either fought or not talked, all the time. They screamed a lot, unable to control their primal reactions. They were lucky that one of them hadn't killed the other. He had wanted to live with her because she didn't want to be owned. He had liked that trait of hers. For a while. Then he found out that it wasn't just a trait. It was a way of life with her. Chris changed buses. The people on this bus were paler. They were headed in a different geographical direction than the last one. The seat was very cold. But it warmed with the heat of her body.

Chris had left Josh behind. Even in little ways. She had bought him a pair of purple pyjamas. He thought them a little fussy. They were beautiful pyjamas. She tried to remember all of what happened on that Saturday. It had been raining. They had made passable love in the morning. Later Josh talked about planting rhubarb. He said that it was easy to grow and that they would have it for years. Years? Years? Bloody years? The cheek of him. But don't say anything. She didn't want anyone — not even Josh — thinking of her in terms of years. Especially when she was in a yearning mood, longing for some verbal or physical passion that would raise this day into one of the greats. Instead they had an argument about why George Eliot had called herself George Eliot. Or rather he said it was a good idea to do so. She said that it was a tragedy. Neither of them became hysterical but Chris felt drained afterwards as if parts of her self were falling dead through lack of use or understanding. The fire was lighting on only one side — a mean sign. Awful things can be said in a cold room. The afternoon dragged on and Josh wanted to be on his own to amalgamate his notes. His very words belonged to a different world now — a place where there were no dreams. He asked her to go out because he found it difficult to concentrate when she was around. He must have — otherwise she would never have gone out at that hour on a Saturday.

She remembered wanting to call on someone. Lil was away. She was always away when you needed her. Noeleen was there but she couldn't handle too personal admissions, and certainly not tears. Noeleen needed to believe that her friends and herself were happy without effort, because if that wasn't the case, what was going to happen next? Vera was there too. But she was vaguely resentful that Chris had not been forced, like herself, into marriage. She also knew that Josh and Chris had often pinned a note on their door 'Back in an

hour,' when they were really in the house. (That was
back in the heady days when friendships could be risked
because the sex was so good.) Vera resented the cheek
attached to this even though she liked most things
about Chris. Who was there that could help, just for a
few minutes? Someone who could put their finger with
her on this vague feeling that something dreadful,
terrible was about to happen. Did she not have any of
those friends left? Hah! And she had taken risks. Josh.
She talked to Josh usually. But what would he say to
this? Nothing. Worse than nothing — he would stroke
the regulation left of centre beard and his eyes would
snap: 'Not again. Don't you know by now that if you
think about something else, or do something, anything,
the feeling will go away?' Anyway what was the point in
talking to him? They couldn't help each other any
further. She had never thought that before. What a
terrible idea. There was still a heavy sadness on her
when she remembered the shock of the realization.
Josh, after all, had been a good man.

That had been the end of it all. That day. That walk.
Not immediately, but Chris was never the same again.
She had thought something that couldn't be ignored. It
was some months before she moved the last of her stuff
out. And she didn't want to think about that again. She
wanted to think about few things. Which was why she
was doing silly things like going to school reunions. And
it hadn't helped any. Stupid of her to think that it would.
She had never got on with that sort of woman. They
were nearly as bad as men.

She looked out the window of the bus at the cold
street and thought of her warm flat, the colour of the
paint and her drama classes. Yes, it was a combination of
the purple pyjamas and the rhubarb. Not really them.
There was something deeper than just them. There
must have been. 'Last stop.' There was Margery putting

out the milk bottles and now closing the gate. She looked like some woman out of a film or a story who looked her best when closing gates.

Home — What Home?

She was sitting on the wooden steps of this cardboard motel trying not to hear the others talk about the heat. The heat. Talking about it helped them — it made her want to cry. They chatted desultorily about degrees — centigrade, fahrenheit, humidity. Dry heat. Hot winds that blew from the desert. Dust. They worked themselves into placid acceptance. She got hotter. Soon someone would say — I could do with a swim. White Australians learned to swim early, sometimes before they walked. They darted around the numerous swimming pools like goldfish, unless it was the backyard pool, which was usually smaller than the local municipal. They moved slowly, carefully around their own backyard pools. They came up for air in wondrous unison all around the coast. They swam in the few feet beside the beach right around this vast continent — always careful to stay nearer the land than the water. Twenty feet out, right around this massive land mass there could be one continuous black line of sharks. That was some comfort to Ellen, who couldn't swim. Some reason for not tackling the problem. How to keep her body up, her lungs empty. She tried. It couldn't be done. How did they do it?

She had lived her life surrounded closer than them by water, but she had never submerged herself. She had looked beyond the sea, never into it. It was Adam who said, 'I think I'll have a dip.' Long slinky Adam. Beautiful body. That's as far as it went, she would imagine. She was sarcastic today. The step was wet under Ellen's legs, where her sweat soaked into the wood. She could think only in monosyllables on days like this. What could she do for the next hot hours, before evening cool came? Somewhere air conditioned. The bar, where else? Then the bus would move off again — off to the football club nightshow, where there was already a block-booking for the passengers. And her. The guide always had to go as well. Some of the holiday-makers might get sick. Some of them might want to make a pass at her. Had to keep them happy. No, she couldn't swim. But she knew their country better than they did and she knew them.

The bar was cool. Bars always were. She drank too much because of that. That was why, or so she told herself. Sometimes doubt asked her if she would drink as much in a cold climate. When, if, she got back to Ireland would the warmth of the bars not seduce her? She ordered a pot. This was Queensland, not New South Wales. Was there a schooner here or not? Thousands of miles of distance was measured in the names of drink measures. No change in accent. None in outlook. Men in Mount Isa talked about the sizes of their women's breasts. Men in Murrimbidgee were equally painfully obsessed. Sydney men wondered what surf was up on which beach this weekend. Men from Cammoweal wondered what surf was up on which Sydney beach this weekend. But they stamped their identities by patenting their drink names. She ordered another midi. One more drink and she would feel much better. The well-being. Odd times, the more she drank the lonelier she got. But not generally. Another midi. This was a good job. It had its advantages.

Ellen had come to Australia because it looked well in the school atlas. Good shape. What better reason? She wanted to see where the Murray and the Darling met. She could never got the confluence quite right on her maps. But she could picture herself standing at the point watching the Murray watching the Darling while the Darling looked back. The day she got there the floods were up and the two rivers were one. They were not meeting. Nothing meets that is one. She also pictured herself riding horseback over the Rockies, wherever the hell she got that fantasy from. She wanted to see Canberra. She saw that too. Between office jobs, and they were plentiful, she moved from city to outback and back, into other cities, into towns, wandering, wandering. For two years she moved, worked, moved again. Now would she go home? No. She had missed something. She must have missed something. She took a job as a tour guide. She would guide white Australians around Australia. Then she would definitely go home. There was Bruce in the corner. He was on the trip because of some family trouble. Divorce probably. She used to stand awed at the panache with which they left their marriages — remember Sue?

'This is my husband, and this is my fiancé.'

'Ex-husband surely,' and it had taken her a long time to trip the word 'ex' off her lips.

'No. The divorce hasn't come through yet.'

Now Ellen scarcely noticed their endless permutations. She hoped that Bruce wouldn't join her. But what man can leave alone a solitary woman? He shuffled himself up and made in her direction. She gulped the last of the Fosters and removed herself, body and mind, to the sparse quarter-room that served as lodging for the night. There she threw herself on the bed to sleep the sleep of the restless until the evening socialities began.

Every Australian set of more than ten houses had a club. If it wasn't the returned serviceman's club it was the younger version, the local football club. Ellen and her passengers were at the junior. Here the men who never had a chance to kill or be killed waited around slot machines for the next war, consoling themselves with sleazy shows, bad singing, drink and waitresses dressed in long dresses, who looked as if they knew exactly what was going on. They tossed their heads in bored semi-acceptance of the ribald comments, then turned to holler, 'Two steaks, medium.' Nothing like that shriek to put a drunk off his line of thinking. Here sat the tour. Disparate people. In Brisbane. Sun-Uppers Number OV 106. And Ellen. An observer could have seen them moving closer, closer as they got drunker. Most unlikely matches caught each other's eyes and stayed there because there was nothing to convince them that they weren't one. Ellen remained apart, aloof. Gary was making great shapes to occupy first her bed, then her heart. She was having none of it. Did he think that he was the first Adelaide boy that she had seen? Did he think that she was on a geographical whuring tour? No thank you, Gary. She mingled with her group, liking the choice that was hers. She could be friendly, close even, tonight. But tomorrow she could sit on the bus poring over maps and hotel reservations, echoing don't come near me I'm busy. And it would work. Because they thought that they depended on her to have a good holiday. She stopped beside the beautiful Adam, who was churning his way through every juvenile joke he could remember. He was very, very drunk. Tottering on collapse, in fact. He's the one tonight, Ellen thought. Wish I could bet with someone that he will get sick. But she could never do that. Never confide in the passengers about one of themselves, especially when the tour was just three days old. That could be the next short-time, life-time partner, wife, husband, lover that you were insulting. For what was the biggest attraction of these tours? After the white gum trees, the cut red gullies, the nature meanderings and the sea, of course. Of course. She moved nearer to Adam. Perhaps if she engaged him in some conversation it might save some trouble later. She saw his tattoo 'Vietnam Who? Me!' Great.

'You're an objector I see.' Ellen smiled at him.

He spun round to her, his face placed inches from hers. 'Whatdidyasay?' He half spat.

'I just wondered if you were an objector. Your tattoo, I mean,' she stammered, shrugging her shoulders as best she could. Tight-lipped, she thought — what did I say that for? He tucked in his eyes, delight gripping his features, as he fixed a glare on her. He was going to have an argument. About his favourite subject. The most recent war.

'Why? Should I be?' he sneered.

Ellen knew. This country divided into moral yes and no steel rods at the mention of Vietnam. How could she have left herself so open to this sneer? But most people would have thought that his tattoo was an objection. Instead it was a birthday present to himself the day he left Sydney Harbour for Saigon. Now she had shown what she thought and there would probably be a large-scale fight. But the passengers around Adam seemed reluctant to carry on the whip. They were on a tour. They had left life behind and had no desire to rush momentarily back to check if it was the same as when they'd departed from it. Most unusually lucky, Ellen mentally thanked them as she eased inches between herself and Adam. She made it to the bar.

The nightshow was over. She was standing counting the passengers on. Adam, she had to admit, was conducting himself admirably considering the amount of beer he had drunk, and the little upset. It could not be easy to be an unwanted veteran. The voices of suburban groups were laughing noisily as they circled their cars. They formed their securities around themselves as best they could with loud remarks and familiar sayings. Too familiar, many a person would think, before the night was out. But what were they to do without their sitting rooms as props behind them? Over-familiarity could be forgiven, social unease never. Ellen's group was quiet by comparison. They were not at home. They would have to see these strangers in the morning. They couldn't push it. Yet. Adam walked toward the bus trying not to look at Ellen but then thought, what the heck, she's only a girl and anyway I like her well enough. Their eyes brushed, flashed what he took to be mutual forgiveness — what the hell, this was a tour. Ellen turned to Gary. She wanted to have a word with him about his refund. He'd been married when he first booked. Now he wanted his wife's share back. Naturally. It might belong to her, but divorce was like that — you picked up the odd hundred here and there. Adam jumped. That was the way the Colonel turned away every morning as they went out. Turn away all the time. Turn away because you mustn't look because you might feel and you might not want to die or send out to die or send out to kill even. She was counting them out to the battlefield. It was the Colonel. No it wasn't. It was the tour guide. No it wasn't. Don't turn from me like that. He got nearer to the bus door. Heavy steps. Light steps. Heavy with fear. Light with fear. He put his foot on the first step and stared straight at the Colonel. You weren't allowed to look like that. He froze in sudden terror. He couldn't move his foot, only his hands, that now flailed out at the bus sides. He wedged both hands, one around the mirror, one around the window catch. He screamed, 'I won't go, I won't go.' He was crying to himself. Screaming to himself. Body wedged by the brute force of his hands to the bus. 'I won't go.' It took the others some minutes to realize what was happening. Then they did all the wrong things. Plead, argue, order.

'It's only a bus Adam, it's only a bus.'

'I won't go,' a silent whimper. 'I won't go. I won't.' Second by second, 'I won't go.'

'Please Adam. Let go of the mirror.'

'It's only a bus Adam.'

'I won't go. What did I do?' A silent whimper.

'It's only a bus.'

'It's the drink, Adam.'

'Bill, be firm with him.'

'Adam! Get on the bus.'

Ellen touched him, a hand between his waist and his hip, her inside arm on his back. She would have preferred to let the men sort it out but they didn't seem to be making much progress. Her flesh warmed into him. He turned, exhausted. It wasn't the Colonel. It was the tour guide. She led him to the front seat. The loud groups were scurrying into their cars, afraid even to stare. The fright of a man crying sent them home quiet. A veteran, at that. Makes for an uneasy world. Ellen's passengers were sober. She sat beside Adam. He looked out the window at Chalk Street, Wooloowin, Fortitude Valley. It was easier than talking.

Sympathy got the better of unease. Back at the hotel Adam flunked again. Quieter this time. It was the only way that he could get to his bedroom through this column of sympathetic or disgusted fellow passengers. Ellen escorted him to his room. Better leave it to her, she had done so well the last time. She hugged him, put him to bed. He talked, staccato like. She went to bed with him like a sister, ignoring his tattoo. Why not? She had been mothered well herself when young and knew what to do. He cried for a long time, like a young brother. Cried, sobbed, slept. Ellen looked at the hotel ceiling, her arm stuck under his heavy head. 'What am I doing here! It was *your* war', she said to the middle of the night. She was too kind to say the obvious. She woke up in the morning feeling used and amused. She looked at the beautiful Adam slunk half across her and wondered what it would be like to be courted by him. Was he too beautiful? He lay pretending to sleep. She knew by the tightness of his eyes that he was holding them shut. To save him the embarrassment of facing her or last night she eased herself from under him onto the hot floor. Hot already. She cursed him — Courageous Boy — and the heat.

Breakfast was as normal. Adam joined them on time. The men pretended that nothing had happened. Some of the women looked openly sympathetic, the fools, then took their cues from the men. Adam pretended that Ellen had slept in her own room. OK, she would forget too. Forget what? No, she should in fact remember. Remember everything. Tell everyone. Announce it from the front of the bus.

'Today we're going to visit the famous war memorial second only to the scrap yard in Canberra. This war memorial ... Adam is impotent. Would all the other impotent men please put up their hands so that the women can be saved the trouble of running after them. Adam, by the way, is terrified as indeed he should be. He's in trouble with himself since Vietnam, as you may have noticed. After that we'll visit the country's first open-air cinema ...'

But that wouldn't be fair. They ate breakfast, all thirty-nine of them (but particularly Ellen and Adam) with the exaggerated caution of those who have been too intimate with strangers. Ellen, talking to all sides of her, finished her breakfast quickly. She was somehow hurt. She collected her maps, her hardback notebook, excused herself and went to talk to the driver. They were doubling back today. Drivers always hated that. She allowed herself one look at the beautiful Adam on the pretext of looking out the window at the weather.

'Today we go to the Gold Coast, some forty kilometres in length. The townships that run into each other include Paradise Point, Surfer's Paradise, Burleigh Heads, Coolangatta.'

Burleigh Heads. Where one night I met eternity. One night and for the rest of my life I will love him. Nothing more, nothing less. And they say that that cannot happen.

'Sorry, where was I?'

Ellen's voice fed easily into the microphone. She would ignore Adam, he would ignore her. She would have herself in control by evening.

'Severe cyclones in the seventies removed much of the sand from the Gold Coast beaches but restoration work has ...'

They were passing through Burleigh Heads. She could have seen the hotel if she had turned her head but she didn't need to. This town, that room, were burning into her body. Her mere eyes did not need to check.

I will love you always. Do you know that? Do you need to know that? She had forgotten Adam. The towns wound their way snakelike into each other, Tallebudgera became Currubim, Tugun-Bilinga swallowed the northern end of Kirra. Only Burleigh Heads remain untouched, solid. They were at Coolangatta, their stop for the day. Go swim your hearts out. No drizzle, no grey water, no vicious Atlantic waves here. Blue Pacific, white surf coming to manageable waves as it laps the last few yards timidly. Cut your way through some inches of that surf and believe that you know the Gold Coast. Adam walked out near the end. He would have liked to wait until everyone else had got off the bus but that would have been much too obvious. He smiled at Ellen.She smiled back. All right, all right, on no account lose an inch, an atom, of your imprisoned manhood for that is all you've got.

The passengers lost themselves in a day of blinding sun, white surf, tan-white sand, deep yellow beer. Ellen thought about why she had left Ireland. Wet grey summers, cold white spring days and the odd warm autumn evening when the holidays were over. She had been reared in that house with three symmetrical eyes looking out on the small hills. There was nowhere else to look. Those hills. She never liked them. They were in the way of other visions. They were all right in themselves, but if she could just move them back a little from the front door her expanse of view could be better. Yes they were much too near the window. She had spent her teenage years reading books and looking for men, boys. There was nothing else to do. She walked down the village suspended in delicious terror until she rounded the corner — his car would be there or not there. Down the town past Patton's. Down to the bus — perhaps he would be sitting in the right seat. The one where she could sit beside him because after all she generally did sit on that side of the bus. Down past the Brothers. Down. Down. Down. All the wrong people loved the wrong people in those young days. Some of them had got so hurt by the ensuing mess that they stopped loving anyone but themselves. On her way to twenty years of age she had observed certain things — the way the shopkeepers and others changed their stance, their tone of voice on meeting their betters. The others, the lessers, might sneer afterwards, but her young eyes saw the humiliations. The shopkeepers and such liked and yearned for the company of their betters, but had to pretend to the lessers that they didn't, that they were one of them. No one believed anyone. They spent their lives circling in one big lie, yet they could discuss the art, the difficulty, especially in wet weather, of grave-digging as if none of them was afraid to die. It would take her years to forget the rooms, the neighbours' faces. The ones she liked, the ones she hated. But still there was something to be said for home. She knew the fields. Every hedge of them. Every tree that stood to give shelter. Every voluptuous hedge that could hide and seat two adults and six children during haymaking showers. Every weather change leaving its mark on them all, human and hedge. The hedges were patched with odds and ends, some from last year's, some from yesterday's work. They would still be the same. Or so she thought. She never dreamt that a new owner might have ripped up every single historical hedge, even the wild white roses, and that there might not be a rush to be seen where previously they had fought with the sparse dry green patches, as they colonized each field.

The village was an old countryman that didn't want to let any of his children out of his grasp because if they went to cities they would change and he would lose them. Cities did strange things to people. Talk with such a variety of people did strange things to their minds. Bruce was standing before her, sand in his hair, his eyes, his mouth. He was singing.

'You have a lovely voice.'

'This I realize.'

She laughed, liking the easy way he took the compliment. His mother was Welsh. They drove back to Brisbane. She closed her eyes tight going through Burleigh Heads, for fear that she would cry.

'Today we go to the Glass House Mountains, a series of steep and massive pillars of trachyte. There are ten principal peaks with numerous outcrops and foothills. They are one of the most striking geological formations in Australia, being volcanic survivals of the Cainozoic Age. Beerwah is 536 metres high and among the other peaks are Coonowrin, Crookneck and Beerburrum.'

Typical. Typical. Beer and crook. One should be called Chunder. Coon. Those quiet black women who made her shiver with their justified hatred of her. White men tried to contain their fear by calling her Coon.

'The peaks present considerable difficulties to the climber, but all have been scaled at different times.'

That would be important. Everything must be climbable.

'The mountains were sighted by Captain Cook in May 1770 and named by him because of their resemblance to the glass furnaces of his native Yorkshire.'

Typical.

What was their real name? How many black women and men had been slaughtered here?

That night in Bundaberg Ellen sat between Sue and Mark. Sue played dumb but occasionally surprised, herself as much as anyone else, with a sharp contribution to the conversation. She suffered the fate unwittingly of women caught in the company of men who cannot decide whether they're big boys or human. Her odd incisive comment proved that she had survived better than most, but her game ensured that she would be loved. Ellen drifted.

There had been so many places. Coff's harbour.

'The town developed into two sections about three kilometres apart — Coff's Harbour and Coff's Harbour Jetty. They have recently merged to form a single urban centre.' Why should she remember there? So many places, so many.

Passengers walking through the Big Pineapple, the Big Banana, monuments to the juicy sweet fruits of their area. Ellen yawned. Sometimes this job wasn't great. Adam was drinking with Bruce. Bruce was in the unenviable position of having been called up but not sent. He drove army trucks of human cargo to and from planes. He could never be either an objector or a veteran. Those were hard lines in this world but he manfully buried his chip and drank with Adam. Ellen went for a drink to the bar. Adam followed her. If she snubbed his tentative suggestion he would order drinks and shrug as if the thought had only momentarily crossed his mind. She took him up on his tentative suggestion. She honestly didn't know why. It could be dangerous, hurtful, boring — but then it might be fun.

They went to Ellen's room. Adam tried to say thanks for the other night without directly referring to it. His stumbling words and naked emotions were painful for Ellen to watch. What could be expected of him? He had been no less gentle than any other boy his age in Goulburn in 1969. He was also very beautiful and felt somehow immune because of that. His mind had gleaned from his body that all would be well with him. He was a simple young man. Or would have been. If all of him hadn't gone with his tattoo. If he hadn't seen the Big White Evil at work in a country that had no latitude or longitude to do with him. But he could be simple again. He could forget. Or so he thought. Ellen perversely wanted to touch the loneliness that he didn't want to know was in him. A loneliness that would be there forever — no matter what he did. He felt better after sex, especially when he managed to perform without blanks. The rest of the tour would be good. For Ellen it would be a drift into a place where she had little control and less satisfaction. But there were no reasons to stop her.

'We are now crossing the Atherton Tableland. This area's red volcanic soil produces one of the best maize crops in Australia as well as valuable timbers including walnut, apple and oak. The tropical jungle, volcanic lakes and rugged ranges attract many visitors. The first settlement took place in 1885 ...'

That means ...

The passengers weren't listening. Adam was asleep, content to be beside the tour guide. Next day they stopped for lunch beside a ghost town. There were streets leading into grass. There were two houses standing, inhabited by people who didn't come to peer at the only outside life that they had seen for months. There had been forty-seven pubs on the street leading west, when the town was a mine, pumping minerals from the earth with a dazzling speed. No bowels were safe from the mine machinery in those days so the earth dried up. Now the town was a museum, preserved in dry heat. Every foot turned up valuable scrap. Signs attached to half house fronts clanged in the windless day, blown by dead spirits that wanted to speak to the tourists, that wanted to say that there had been life here once so don't be so cocky. She shouldn't have brought them to this graveyard, and yet Ellen was drawn to the old creaking signs. She didn't know them, had never been acquainted with them during lifetime but they comfortably reminded her of the shiny seat on an old mowing machine that was yearly being buried by growth in an orchard in Ireland. She used to slide her bottom over it, thinking about all sorts of things — everything except the machine. Nonsense — these signs were not like that machine. Yet it was scrap too. She would have to admit that. And her unspoken memories were there, as words said or written, to keep mowing machines and loved pieces of scrap metal alive. She was right to bring them here. She lay passive that night hoping that Adam knew what the hell he was doing down there because she certainly didn't. If she had been different she might have known what to say. If she had been from some different part of the world.

But Ellen simply lay, sad and unmoved. He sensed her uninterest and pleaded that he could do nothing more than learn from her. If she had been someone else she might have thought — fat lot of good that is, but instead she acquiesced in his inability and said that she was sorry.

Ellen treated Normanton, Cloncurry, Mount Isa, Alice Springs and the thousands of flat red miles that separated them with the awe and respect due to places that survived such heat and loneliness. The passengers wondered why they had never learned such words at school. In Mount Isa she had slipped away from them to spend an evening in an Irish club. She had worked in this town before. There were people here who came to make new lives, new money. But behind them there were women and men who had secret passions for self-communion. They had chosen red dust, bindies and startling heat as their life surroundings rather than softer familiar places. They tried not to write home about the lemon trees in the back garden because they did not wish to boast. Then there were the oranges, the refrigerated air-conditioning, and all the other ... so soon they couldn't write at all. They were forgotten and in time they forgot. Ellen had been reluctant to leave them but the tour — the crazy journeyings of uneasy people through places — had to be serviced.

She conveyed her feelings about people who felt duty-bound to climb Ulurhu, (and to misname it Ayer's Rock), but still the passengers climbed it, some to the top. She would have sat in its shadow wondering about the drawings, about what the aborigines thought of her and them as they bundled out to see the sun rise and set on a stone that held none of their secrets.

So they continued their tour, Ellen imparting information and personal feeling through the microphone each day. She and Adam had occasional sex and less occasional conversation. Sometimes they lay awake on the same night longing for some gentle word but neither of them understood the other's loneliness on nights like that. One Thursday they came to a prison. Wentworth Prison, named after a man who believed in kindness to convicts. The bricks were made by the convicts themselves, then placed one on top of the other, line by line, around the gables until all the space and air was captured. They must have wanted the process to slow. The day they finished the prison they were locked up inside their own bricks. Ellen handled the book of escapees. She read the names Murphy, McCann and others. Big county men — six foot three, six foot one, five foot eleven. Their ages — approximately thirty. Their private marks. Birthmark on inside of left thigh. Blue mole behind the ear. Simple brands by which to recapture them. She saw hundreds of men with damp hearts from inward crying. Tears going down their throats through their lungs wetting their hearts as they remembered who they were and never would be again. Better to make some sort of break no matter what the risk, even though that air out there beyond the bricks would never be home — hadn't you tasted it? Ellen couldn't afford to get too sentimental about that. Not because of the group — they would have loved it. Because of herself.

Once he cried, drunk, that he felt that he wasn't making any progress, that he would never understand. She told him, drunk, that the world was as it was. He should view it with a long glance and intervene only if he thought that someone was listening to him. That would bring him happiness. He listened to this advice with corrosive skepticism. He had not been allowed to have such a pedestrian consumer view of life so far. Neither had she, but she liked to pretend.

They came back to Sydney as different people from those who had left it. Some of them were changed inside, some had merely acquired unconnected evidence of knowledge, some had only acquired souvenirs, some of *them* as minute as the Book of Australian Toilets. What now, Adam asked, as the bus pulled into the depot, and because she didn't know either, and was afraid not to know, they got a flat together.

Ellen knew Sydney. Little lanes with offices. She had walked here looking for jobs. That office there, between the big ones. Maybe they would need her. The shop beside the milk-bar. Maybe they would need her. She wouldn't ask at the milk-bar because she would have to shop there every day. The club on the car-park. Coles, maybe. She was ferrying over the harbour, going for an interview. She wasn't seeing the boats, the Opera House, the Bridge, the sails, the beauty. She was remembering her sister's twenty-first. She had worn a pink linen dress with a zip down the front. The sleeves were ruffled nylon, paler pink. What matter what she wore? It distressed her that she remembered. Now to make matters worse she was wondering if her sister remembered. She got the job. Later she got ready to go to some forgettable club. She let the blue dust fall from around her fingers, one eye closed as she brushed it lovingly over the lid. Blink. Tidy up the corner. Now the other eye. Blink. Tidy. Make equal. Stand back to look. Two index fingers doing half moon circles, starting from exactly the same point give symmetry. Blusher. A narrow ivory box, fat in the middle, with a square inch mirror under the cover. Smell. The smell of mother's powder puff. Reasonable mother. She had patted a paler powder, on her nose only, just to take the shine away and to cover up the tadpole blue veins that lay faintly below her skin reminding her of other deeper matters. Ellen brushed pink gold blusher on her cheek bones, furiously, inhaling the smell. The colour added height to her face. Her eyes were surprised. She moved closer to the mirror, closed one eye and curled her lashes around the curling stick. Her eyes darkened and heavied. Beautiful. No lipstick. She laid a hand on the table and shaped and reshaped the nails, blowing all the time as the file altered nail matter to dust. Then the other. Varnish. Clear varnish. It painted on, then glistened. She could dance her nails together later and they would glide off each other because of this varnish. Her watch. Her bracelet. A simple bracelet. It made a noise when she moved her hand. A private sound — a personal extra — that gave her confidence in difficult moments. Earrings, bright earrings, barely showing below her hair. Her ring. The precious cheap red stone ring that had been on her finger since she was twelve, as if she had no responsibility for it. The rituals were not at all for anyone else. They were offerings known only to herself that were a connection with a former self. Would this getting ready lead her back to her sisters? It would be a wide evening at home. The blue, grey and black stretching forever. The clouds doubling up as cities in the sky. There would be pink light coming through select clouds. For any child, these would be God's houses. The wide stretches would be the road to heaven. Would a different job help? No. Ellen would have to go home.

Adam did not understand. Hadn't he been good to her? He wasn't impotent any more? What did she want?

Ellen took off her halter neck and the sticker 'Make

love Not babies' from the back of her trousers and went home.

Once Upon
a Time

I'm not quite sure which of the gods it was but it was one of them anyway. God the father, the son, the ghost, Gabriel, Michael, how would I be expected to know which of them it was. They're all wearing the same colours in the one inappropriate place as far as I'm concerned. But it was one of them. Now that I think about it a bit more I'm nearly sure that it was god the father. Anyway he was writing a story.

*   *   *   *

He was taking his time at it. No rush at all. All the time in the world. He was writing about this woman Moira. A woman who wouldn't stay with her husband. Come to think of it he wasn't her husband at all but in light of worse things he was. God knew how he wanted to do it. He was going to build the scenes, fluff it out a bit, use long weighty sentences, and in the end he was going to teach her a lesson. He hadn't worked out yet what this lesson would be, but he'd come up with something to save her soul. He started writing. But the craziest thing happened to god. Someone else took over the story. He couldn't control his pen. He was sitting in his chair. His hand and new biro were moving, but those weren't his words that were coming out. He was being drawn down down down into a car, on a road, on earth, to a woman. Her name was Moira.

It was a strange evening, the sort when unexpected things can happen. There was no particular chill in the air even though a black frost waited in the sky. But it let god through first, before it began to descend. Moira was driving her car home, staring ahead, unsurprised at god's sudden presence. She had in fact invited him down. Her car was falling apart but still it kept going. 'It's more faithful than a dog,' she said, in between singing to herself and deliberately singing to the children. Her song was a form of prayer. The children took turns to join in, humming incoherently. The oldest, who was four, looked at her mother sometimes — a short look — wondering, wondering, then went back to hitting the yellow brick off the red one in the fashion of men who pull bits out of their beards. (She barely noticed god and certainly took no notice *of* him). She seemed interested in her mother, or in something about her, or in something different that had happened recently. Like the three of them talking on the way home every evening (although you couldn't call those noises from the babyseat talking) and her singing all those songs, instead of screaming at them. Something different is right, which is exactly why god was here. He was a strange sort of man this god, he was thinner than she expected.

'But it's wrong,' he said. (He had decided to ignore the original problem about the validity of this marriage.)

'Not at all,' she said, 'that was long ago when all of you thought that women were just slaves and you all made the rules anyway because you had to cover up about Eve.'

'What about Eve?' he said.

'You know, and don't pretend you don't. The frame up, the scapegoating.'

'Hmmm,' he said.

'It was very different then, and we have new ways now. We're getting our nerve although it's hard. For one thing we never really believed you — WHERE were all the women? What did they say? You didn't even have the women saints saying anything. So!' 'So,' she said again, as if that settled that.

He would have to find some way to stop her but he could only say 'I see . . .'

'Sing the one about the blowing train,' the four-year-old asked and Moira sang it. She was pleased that the child remembered even though that song always reminded her of evenings when she had been married and had driven home, as she always did then, to the quiet restless turmoil that was as Siamese brother to the eternal boredom that she was told she must now endure forever. OK, so she wasn't married now but she could still remember what it was like, if she felt like it, and she sometimes did just that to make her thankful for new days.

'It was an ordinary evening of two years ago, but I remember it particularly now because it was the same evening as this one. An evening of cold dew in the country and placid tempers, these evenings that happen without warning.'

The children and god listened. It was indeed a strange carload. Historical, you could say. A mother, a god, a four-year-old girl, and a baby boy.

'That evening the oldest child was sulking, holding her breath preparing to lash out any minute. The waiting is always the worst. The youngest was scratching at the air with pointless screeches that frayed the edges of my nerves.' God had not known any of this before and he could feel her thinking badly of him for his ignorance. 'I was speeding home to cook the tea. There wasn't much food in the house because *I* had forgotten to get it.' God had never known that mothers forgot to get food. He grimaced. She glared at him. 'I was trying to think what I'd make out of scraps of meat. We have to endlessly think on these things, continuously clog our minds up with scraps of meat and the like, I ask you.' She turned up her nose. 'Scraps of meat can ruin the best of thoughts. I had stayed an extra half hour talking to Jean.' (Indeed they had. They had even talked, without rancour or coarseness — the helpless are rarely coarse or rancorous — about how the world, not just the sun, always shone on men.) But that wasn't dawdling, was it? 'I often got the impression that I was being punished. Strange feeling that.' Jean and Moira often said little things, safe little things, that brought themselves and each other comfort, but they never complained directly about their own husbands. That would be a dangerous thing to start.

Now it would be such a rush to get tea in time. Moira had gritted her teeth and sunk her shoe. The car speeded up, rushing not to anywhere worthy of the speed but to the semi-D that would be freezing for at least an hour after she got the fire lit. She got to the driveway, cold and panicked. She hurried the children in — lugging in that precious you've had a daughter and you've had a son as if they were bags of rotten potatoes — changed a nappy, put on the dinner, vegetables, potatoes, the scraps of meat pounded into tasteless burgers, lit the fire, set the table. The children fought bitterly in the still cold room about who owned the tin drum. The tin drum that never failed to cause hysterics. She must get rid of it. Tonight. Pat came in.

God said, 'Yes. Now don't you see.'

'See what?' she smiled abstractedly. 'We kissed. I sometimes wondered why we did that. It was such a pointless ritual. I was angry. Why this evening? This was the same as any other evening. But time is like that — it makes itself felt for no apparent reason. By the time the children were in bed I was shaking with uncontrollable rage. I wanted to lash out at Pat, to sting him, to make him suffer too, but it is too difficult to fight your corner when first you have to prove that there are corners.'

God tried to interrupt, 'But it's a sin.'

She raised her voice, 'Get away out of that. Pat talked about the great extension that was being built onto Doyles' house. He hadn't seen it before this evening, which he said was funny, because it was nearly finished. That was that. I knew that now he was started this would be the topic of conversation for the evening. I knew that if I wanted to make myself understood I would have to say some terrible things. My dear god, you would have been surprised. I don't think you really understand women. Anyway it was easier to talk about Doyles' extension. So I discussed the important question of how much Pat and I could afford to spend on an extension all of our own. Not as much as the Doyles. Do you understand, god? Do you understand? We went to bed and I pretended that I was asleep so that Pat would go to sleep. He did. Then I cried. Those times I cried a lot, over nothing really and everything. My thoughts, my poor dear thoughts, laid now in the foundations of a new extension. It was always the same. And there was nothing I could do. Nothing. Nothing.

God stalled her, 'But . . .'

'So in the end it was sin or me. The evenings, too many weeks, the years were too much for me.'

God got his chance, 'But you can't. You can't do that. It's a sin.'

'Hah!' she said. 'You're beginning to sound like an

old gramophone. You gave me a head. What did you want me to do with it? Abuse it? Unuse it? Sit in the house collecting things, staving off thoughts of death? You wanted me to procreate out of hate. What would the women saints have to say on *that?*'

Ah! yes. He understood. But it put him in an awful flummox. What could he do now? Perhaps she wouldn't say it to anyone else? He went silent.

Moira sang the song about the blowing train again. The three of them could take their time getting home this evening — presumably god wouldn't come with them the whole way.' There was no hurry because there was no one waiting for HIS tea. So she stopped the car and they went for a walk. The children loved the air, just the air, the way children love things without knowing them. And the clumps of noisy leaves. Moira loved time. Long ago when her very hours belonged to someone else she would not have understood this. God walked with her. They were comfortable enough together but there was nothing more to be said. They got back into the car. She came to an intersection, where a bully was trying to force his way past her. 'Drive on,' said god. 'Who the hell does he think he is just because he has got a big car!'

*   *   *   *

He got out at the next lights and waved.

Park-going Days

They took their chairs and children, of whom they were terribly proud today, to the park on the first day of summer, relieved that the darkness was over and repeating again and again great day so that maybe such sunworship would bring them a summer. You would never have believed that in those few houses there could be so many children — you could easily have forgotten Kathleen's fifth or that Bridie during the winter had had another because naturally you never saw it, Bridie's new one, due to the freezing conditions. If you did Bridie was a bad mother and there were no good or bad mothers around here, (even the ones whose sons were inside) — just mothers. It was a Thursday after dinner — the one man who had a job nearby had been fed — no one would have gone to the park before that happened, not in deference to Jack eating but because Jack's wife wouldn't be free until then and there was nothing to make a woman feel housebound like all the other women trooping up to the park before her and there was nothing worse than feeling housebound on a sunny day.

The park-going days of sunshine were truly numbered in this country — fifteen last year, two the year before, ten the year before that and forty on the year that god was otherwise occupied and forgot to switch off the heat or else decided to tease us and make us mournful for the next five years. No woman in this country had any doubt but that god was a man — *is* a man. There's no was about that fellow unfortunately. Some had the view that the man himself was intrinsically all right and that it was the ones who took over after him who mucked the whole thing up. Could be true — he may have been all right. Perhaps. But it's a hard thing to believe in a country that only once had forty days of sunshine. It's amazing the amount of pre-parations women used to working can put into a trip to the park. One folded up light deck chair, suntan oil, face cloth, sandwiches which will avoid having to make a children's tea at six, rug to put sandwiches and children on, sunglasses, small lightish jumpers in case it turns cold suddenly, drinks, the anti-biotics that the child is on, some toys for the baby — for the ones who were pregnant last summer — the baby's bottle, one nappy and ALL that baby stuff, *and* ice cream money.

At ten past two all the doors opened and out they poured nearly invisible behind all the paraphernalia, calling around them the children who had been dreamy and inside and the ones who had already been outside getting burned and thirsty and cranky. And dirty.

'Look at the face of her. Come here to me until I give you a wipe. Disgracing me.' She dug the facecloth into the child's face disgracing her in front of friends who hadn't noticed at all.

They went and Rita went after them not to the park but past the park on the way to the shops, half hoping that if there was a summer next year, or if this one lasted beyond the day, that they would ask her to join them, knowing that it would be better if they didn't because if they ran out of steam — which they would when they realised the sort of her and why — there could be no more casual comments passed between them as strangers. They and she could whistle pleasantries back and forth at the moment, they prepared to waste their sweet words on her because of curiosity — (a new resident) — she to make them less curious, and failing.

The more she said nice day the more they wanted to know. The more she felt their sniffing the more frightened she got. That sneaky-faced woman in the nylon housecoat, too old to walk to the park, polishing her brasses again. Who did she think she was fooling? Of course she was lonelier than if she was dead but Rita couldn't set her sympathy juices working.

Rita walked after them aggravated at the bits and pieces of garages built at the ends of gardens as if thrown together in shapeless anger. In winter she could escape them by looking down at her feet, which she did, but today the sun threw their shadow across the street under her eyes. A bulldozer was needed badly. Knock the whole lot of them. She had no soft spots for old farm barns, mudwall byres or extended hen houses so she couldn't see anything for them but the bulldozer. Her husband would not have agreed. But then he came from places where fields lay companionably beside other fields that ran casually into more and more fields, flat and hilly, offering place grudgingly to the occasional house that was then forced to use rickety outhouses as protection against the ever-approaching grass. She was from a geometrician's dream where back gardens were only concessions to the superior needs of houses. She passed the park and saw them.

They belonged to a time before the time of one earring. Two ears, two earrings. Fingers were the only single part of them that divided into ones. They put rings on them, most importantly they put one ring on one finger sometimes along with another varying in degrees of vulgarity and awfulness. The rings marked stages in their self denial and destruction. Rita saw the rings glistening in the sun picking out unreachable baubles in the sky. They saw her and thought different things none of them actually about her, more about her type.

'You couldn't satisfy *him*. If it's not the smog, it's the dirt or the accents. Jayzus would yeh listen to whose talkin' about an accent.'

'How *does* she put up with him? An' it's made her odd.'

'There's somethin' else odd about her but I can't put me finger on it.'

'Ah well.'

In the end they knew in their hearts that the only thing funny about her was that they didn't know her and that she was married to a culchie. Not much of a gap to be got over.

They settled in their chairs and watched their collective new generation comparing it favourably with the other groups in the park, conscious that they were all part of even more park groups, between them accounting for hundreds of miles of discarded umbilical cords.

They uttered unconnected sentences at random. Conversation was organised only when there was tragedy or scandal to be related. But the silence was never silent, it was just a space of time between words of explanation and more words of inadequate explanation.

Bridie watched hers out of the corner of her eye, Sean always dirty. As a baby he sucked the ends of his babygro and got a red wrist in his fat little cracks from wet aggravation. Now he sucked his jumper and pulled at his waist all the time ending up each evening with handmarks branded in frustration on his clothes. His pores seemed to suck in every bit of street dirt going. His cuts usually went septic. Anne. Wise. Precocious and clean. Wise as the wound. She would have children too — it didn't bear thinking about. She played with her older brothers in a superior bossy way as if she knew.

'She'll be coming out of school at half two when she makes her communion, please god.'

That would be another step passed in the sending off of her to the Lord.

'It took me all day to get out of town yesterday. Pickets outside the Dáil. They should put that buildin' down the country somewhere and not be stoppin' people tryin' to get home. They wouldn't be so quick to picket it if it was down there.'

They shifted their fat bodies around on the deck chairs. They had suffered from the usual emotional disappointments being married to their husbands. Kathleen's man had been mortified one day when she was nearly due and she'd sat down on the steps of the bank in town, not fit to move another inch. It was a Saturday and the bank was closed, what *could* he have been going on about? In her early marriage before having any, Molly used to call on her husband at work. She thought it was a nice thing to do and she was lonely on her own — she'd been getting eleven pounds before the wedding, now with tax it was only five, so there wasn't much point in her going to work for the short while, the bus fare was two pounds. One day he said that she'd have to stop calling and get used to their new house for both their sakes. The men at work would start talking.

'But I don't know anyone.'

'You'll get to know some mothers later.'

He smiled. She smiled. It was a small subtle exclusion, preparation for the major ones — the tapping on the shoulder as women walked absentmindedly, not deliberately, not provokingly, into supermarkets pushing prams. She never called again. Bridie's man, when he was young, had kept running from one country to the other filling himself up with experience, pouring himself all over the continent and still he hadn't one word to say for himself. He'd only said once I love you. He was a consumer of cultures — he had a few words of French which gave him an edge on the other men on the street but that was no help to Bridie. Susan's man — the drinker — did his bit for his children. He talked about them occasionally in pubs in the serious way that drunk men do, once getting first day issue covers for them from a man who worked in the P & T who happened, just happened, to be drinking beside him. Now that was more than a woman could do. Kathleen had broken her mother's heart — Ma I wasn't going to tell you this but seeing we're out for the day and that it's on my mind and I have been keeping it to myself and all that and it's no good for me or anything and all that and no good for you either and I'm pregnant. Kathleen sighed. Bridie put her varicose veins on the wheel of the pram. These — the fat, the veins, the sighs — were the shapes of the backbone of the country. You'd never think it to see the corkscrew frown-free pictures that poured from the admen's anorexic fantasies.

'Great day.'

'A doctor said to my mother once that there are two terrible bad things for a woman, ironing and not dropping everything to run outside when she sees the first blink of sun.'

'Yeah, it's a great day.'

'I'd like a cigarette. Funny the way you feel like it sometimes and not at others.'

'I didn't know you smoked Molly.'

Molly raised her voice to panic pitch.

'Smoke. Smoke is it? I was a chain smoker. What! I had meself burnt. Me lips, me skirts, me bras, me slips. One match would do me the whole day. Lit one off the other.'

'What did you smoke?'

It was neither a question nor a statement after Molly's emotion.

'Albany'.

'Were they a special cigarette, I don't remember them. I

used to smoke Woodbine. No one ever died that smoked Woodbine.'

'It's near tea-time.'

That was a grand day. No one had got cut or desperately badly hurt. There had been the odd row but not enough to deserve a beating. One woman, not belonging to their group, had set her child up for a battering. She hit her because she wanted to go on the swings too often. The child kicked her back. The women nodded a sort of ungrudging serve you right nod. The mother hit her more. The incident might have spiralled into murder but the floating disapproval, the soul sympathy, and the take-it-easy-it'll-get-better thoughts made the mother acknowledge defeat. Yes, a great day.

They were gathering up their stuff when Rita walked past on her way home. They delayed, to let her go on. They were sick of her kind, really, never any children, coming to live in that rented house, teasing their curiosity and staying aloof.

'You wouldn't mind so much marrying a culchie but getting *used* to him.'

They laughed. They could have remarked that she was unhappy but they denied her that status in the mean way that city people can, surrounded as they are by so many, some of whom, precisely because of the number, are dispensable. They turned their noses up and pulled their curtains down an inch from their faces like country wans could never do. (Perhaps you might need her in twenty years when all the rest would be gone, to America, or Dublin.) As they struggled nearer their doors, exhausted from heat, children whinging, when *they* saw the prospect of home looming closer, that they hadn't stayed long enough in the park, only three hours Mammy; they each withdrew themselves from collective experience and concentrated on their individual problems. Parks were all right — open-air sum totals of lives that were normally

lived in box rooms with thick enough doors and walls to
shut out obscenities — but all the same you wouldn't want
to live in a park all your life and you wouldn't want to
behave in your own house as if you were in a park. After a
while people get on your nerves, even on sunny days — that
was why the tenants in the rented house were always
handy. Everyone on the street could take their collective
spite against each other out on them and so avoid major
street fights.

Rita knew what they were thinking. Sometimes at
four in the morning — she often woke at four — she would
look out and see reflections of their lights and she would feel
like forgiving them because who couldn't forgive a woman
anything when they saw her struggling at that unearthly
hour to silence a crying, hungry baby. Rita *had* had a child of
her own. The child had died and she wasn't allowed to think
about it. What had happened was anyone's guess — it just
died. But Rita was fine now. Fine. The street would have
gushed with sympathy if it had known. One thing Rita
regretted not having was park days with mothers. She'd
noticed the way mothers made up to the children on park
days. Made up to them for all sorts of troubles, things like
concentrated compressed family violences that emptied
onto children's backsides when men and women decided at
the same moment that they would have to put manners on
the offspring who was at that second holding their nerves
to ransom. They could do that because they knew that
mothers would make it up sometime soon — certainly in a
park if it was a sunny day. Rita would have liked the making
up bits.

It was Bridie in the end who asked Rita if she wanted to
sit down with them in the park just for a few minutes, for a
little rest. She stretched her legs out in front of her and said
to herself now I'll have to leave. They talked busily as they
watched the replay of yesterday and yesterday. Rita not
thinking all the time of her own because she wasn't allowed

to, each of the other women remarking to herself how nice she was really. The next day it rained. Clouds stalked over the bit of sunshine they'd had and Rita started packing. She said goodbye before herself and her culchie husband left, knocked on the single doors and got away before they learned anything about her. A week later if you could have cut bits out of the walls you would have seen them bending over the baby in the way that causes bad backs, cleaning noses, swiping at bare legs, sneaking off for a rest and drying clothes, again, again, as the tenants moved in and the rain poured on them all.

Susan — Did You Hear…

I am so worried. I have seen that man again. Over there. See. Everywhere I go I see him. Who me? No, I'm not paranoid. Well if it's not him it's someone terrible like him, I can tell you. Always I insult him, eventually, and I dust my coat, usually the collar, as I turn my back on him, confident that I'll never see him again. But here he is now again tonight. See. Over there. In the corner. Stand on your toes. Get up on my shoulders if you need to — of course you can stand on my shoulders; it's no one else's business. He's the one in the grey. Yes — him. He's the fellow I was telling you about.

'Not him. He doesn't look the type.'

Susan, they never do. They never do. I must put on my glasses. I can't see him properly. Well if it's not him it's his double. See the man beside him. I went out with him once.

'Once, or once upon a time?'

I was mad about him. Then I lived with him for years, well metaphorically anyway. We side-stepped the volcanoes that stirred below my minor insults. I harnessed my every thought, while I was with him, and never let one of them out beyond the back of my forehead. I was afraid. Actually I was married to him but don't let on to anyone.

'Would you not like to speak to him now? If you were married and all that?'

Naw. Naw. I don't think so. Not much point really. He hates me and maybe he shouldn't be blamed for that. See the fellow beside him? Did I ever tell you that he raped my sister? Once. No, not my blood sister. Yes — him — the one with the red beard and the velvet jeans. She hasn't been the same since. Hasn't he a lovely jacket! I like the tie. It would look nice tightened a bit more, don't you think. In the courtroom he cut her heart out slowly. You wouldn't think it to look at him, would you? Her innards had been cut out during the rape itself. She bled for months after it — and then her heart. She said that her heart going was nearly worse than her insides being torn around. I said that I found that hard to believe but then I've never been raped. The man beside him defended him in court.

'But they're drinking together! They're friends! They're drinking pals!'

I know, Susan, I know. Sometimes you can be awfully naive. If you were a rapist wouldn't you get your drinking buddy to defend you too?

'Ummm. It's just that I didn't expect that rapists would have any kind of friends. And certainly not solicitors or barristers or doctors or anything like *that.*'

God, Susan, you are naive. Hello Patrick. How are you?

'Who's he?'

My landlord. Metaphorically speaking. He doesn't own an inch of space around me. But he struts as if he's holding something up his sleeve. Something like, what happens dearie when you can't pay the rent? But I'm sure, love, that we can come to some arrangement. I'd kill him sooner than touch him. I'm sure he'd be surprised to hear that.

'But you're smiling at him.'

Naturally, Susan. Naturally. What do you expect me to do? Look glum all the time? That fellow in the blue talks very loud doesn't he? Boasting about the brothels he's been to, I suppose . . .

'You're too hard sometimes.'

Not at all. Not at all. Hello again Patrick. How are you? Susan WHAT are you doing with my ribs? Sorry, what did you say? Oh my God! You're joking. You poor thing. We'll ignore him. He'd only love it if you left now. We'll sit tight here and pretend he's not happening. You keep looking at me and I'll keep talking to you until you've got yourself relaxed. Do you want another cigarette? Are you all right pet? See the fellow coming in the door . . .

'You don't know him as WELL!'

I do. Metaphorically, of course. He was lethal during his menopause and the fellow with him — he has . . .

'No. No. I can't stay here. Please. Please. Let's go next door. It's bound to be better.'

Susan, you're joking. It's worse in there.

'Why don't you do something about it? You know who these men are.'

Susan, darling, what would you like me to do? Shoot them all here and now? It would be very very messy. You might get sick. And you would be the very first to complain about the carpet. I can just hear you — how will we get the stains out of the new carpet. The NEW carpet. Hello Patrick. How are you?'

DIFFERENT KINDS OF LOVE
A Collection of Short Stories
Leland Bardwell

Leland Bardwell is well established as a writer of novels, but in this her first collection of short stories we discover how an extraordinary talent can move with ease from one distinct genre to another. Her wonderfully creative style brings, with illuminating vividness, a sense of empathy with each of her characters. Here too we see stories of struggle as the author brings to life a world of poverty and violence; a world where the spirit of Anne Lovett is evoked and a world where we see the affinity of women's lives crossing the rural and urban gap.

ISBN 0 946211 34 5 (pb) £3.95   ISBN 0 946211 35 3 (hb) £10.00

WOMEN IN FOCUS
Contemporary Irish Women's Lives
Pat Murphy and Nell McCafferty

Women in Focus presents a unique visual documentation of contemporary Irish women's lives. It consists of over 100 images preselected by the photographers themselves.

Women in Focus combines portraiture with action and presents a mix of photographers work drawn from the creative, community and journalistic areas. The excitement, energy and vitality captured here makes *Women in Focus* a highly unusual and visual publication.

The outbreak of women in the arts is recognised as one of the most influential forces of the 80s. Cultural activity in Ireland would appear to be taking on a new strength. The activism of the 70s and 80s has diversified into many areas of Irish social and political life. *Women in Focus* portrays women as actively involved in this period of change.

The implications and impact of these photographs are addressed by Pat Murphy and Nell McCafferty. Pat Murphy, film-maker, brings her visual interpretative response to *Women in Focus*, analysing its contents both politically and visually. Nell McCafferty, undoubtedly Ireland's leading journalist and writer, brings her very unique and personal response in only the way Nell can.

ISBN 0 946211 30 2 £9.95 (pb)   ISBN 0 946211 31 0 £19.95 hb

MS MUFFET AND OTHERS
Fairy Tales for Feminists

Ms Muffet and Others is the second in our collection of fairy tales for feminists. The first, *Rapunzel's Revenge*, was highly acclaimed for its originality and style.

Told from a feminist perspective, *Ms Muffet and Others* is a unique collection of fairy tales and fables. Each writer presents, what was the traditional, in an unorthodox and challenging way. The nine contributors, including Maeve Kelly, Leland Bardwell, Liz McManus, Evelyn Conlon and Máirín Johnston, cover a broad spectrum of literary talent, moving from the straight, or even crooked humour of *The Woodcutter's Daughter,* to the sensitive and evocative language of *The Selkie.*

The critics were unreserved in their praise for *Rapunzel's Revenge,* and will, without doubt, receive *Ms Muffet and Others* with the same enthusiasm.

'*Rapunzel's Revenge,* a funny, sassy, heretical collection of fairy tales.'   *Irish Times.*

ISBN 0 946211 272 £3.50 $6.50 pb   Illustrated
64pp. Size: 6" × 8¼"

RAPUNZEL'S REVENGE
Fairy Tales for Feminists

'*Rapunzel's Revenge* is a feminist re-writing of fairy tales which has Mary Maher revealing that Snow White organised the seven dwarfs into a trade union, Maeve Binchy exposing Cinderella's prince as a foot fetishist, and a truly gifted Joni Crone showing that feminist fairy tales can be written in fairy tale language. Wendy Shea's cartoon of Little Ms Muffet, saying to the spider 'C'mon, baby, frighten me to death' should be framed'.

In Dublin.

'Things will never be the same again down in the woods ... Maeve Binchy, Carolyn Swift, Mary Maher and several others give a sardonic feminist twist to the fairy tales we all grew up on.
Sunday Independent.

'*Rapunzel's Revenge,* a funny, sassy, heretical collection of fairytales...'   *Irish Times.*

ISBN 0 946211 18 3 £3.50 $6.50 pb   Illustrated
64pp. Size: 6" × 8¼"

PERSONALLY SPEAKING
Women's Thoughts on Women's Issues
edited by Liz Steiner-Scott

Personally Speaking is a time bomb, and it is the only kind of time bomb I can imagine ever having a creative and positive outcome. When it goes off in the minds of women, it will break through invisible walls of isolation, help women to recognise their own power and release a great deal of healthy energy ... It has already become my handbook ... I feel I am in the company of women who understand and with whom I empathise.

June Levine *Southside.*

'I found the majority of the essays provocative and persuasive ... accessible and clearly written. The book is guaranteed to spark off lots of lively (and heated) debate'.   *New Hibernia.*

'To be honest I thought it was just another woman's book until I burned the midnight oil reading many of the contributions ... However, this is different — 22 different women writers, of all ages, background and opinions have been skilfully gathered together between the covers of this new book and it is at once provocative, interesting, annoying and gives a marvellous picture of how Irish women feel about a variety of topics'.

Maureen Fox, *Cork Examiner.*

'At last we have the beginnings of a native feminist anthology'.
In Dublin.

ISBN 0 946211 108 £5.95 $8.95 pb   ISBN 0 946211 094 £12.95 $24.95 hb
304pp. Size: 5" × 7½"

WOMAN TO WOMAN
A Health Care Guide and Directory
Anne Roper

Woman to Woman is the first broad based health handbook to be published for women in Ireland. Until now Irish women have had to look further afield for information on health issues. This book looks at all the main health topics of concern to women — menstruation, sexuality, mental health, violence, reproduction and contraception, as well as those relating to positive health care — diet, exercise, alternative health care and body image. *Woman to Woman* also includes a comprehensive thirty-two county directory of all groups, organisations and individuals involved in the area of health care in Ireland.

Most health guides are written like text books with highly technical language. *Woman to Woman* is different. This uniquely illustrated book presents basic information in a clear and accessible way. Be it on the issue of sex/sexuality, menopause, violence or mental health *Woman to Woman* deals with each subject in an informative and interesting way.

'When two women meet the subject of health is often discussed, we ask questions, compare facts, and respond to each others anxieties. We use the question and answer format routinely.' For this reason *Woman to Woman* has followed that model, each chapter contains an introduction followed by a series of questions and answers — questions commonly asked by women, yet so often unanswered.

Woman to Woman is of relevance not only to the young maturing woman, but also to women who are learning to cope with the changes that come with age.

A main feature of *Woman to Woman* is the comprehensive index which allows quick cross referencing and easy access to any information you require.

ISBN 0 946211 23X £5.95 $8.95 pb   ISBN 0 946211 248 £12.95 $24.95 hb Illustrated
256pp. Size: 5¾" × 8¼"